# LATTER RAIN

# LATTER RAIN

## VANESSA MILLER

**URBAN
CHRISTIAN**

*www.urbanchristianonline.net*

Urban Books
1199 Straight Path
West Babylon, NY 11704

ISBN- 13: 978-1-60162-979-1
ISBN- 10: 1-60162-979-6

First Printing February 2009
Printed in the United States of America

10   9   8   7   6   5   4   3   2   1

Distributed by Kensington Corp.
Submit Wholesale Orders to:
Kensington Publishing Corp.
C/O Penguin Group (USA) Inc.
Attention: Order Processing
405 Murray Hill Parkway
East Rutherford, NJ  07073-2316
Phone: 1-800-526-0275
Fax: 1-800-227-9604

# Acknowledgments

My daughter, Erin, is one of my biggest supporters. I am so grateful for her love and support. My family and friends have helped spread the word about the Rain Series, and I want to thank them for that. But most of all, I have to thank my mother. Mrs. Patricia Harding is my road buddy. We've traveled through hurricanes and tropical storms. We've had a car battery die on us in Nashville and in Indianapolis. We almost drove into oncoming highway traffic one sleepy night en route home from New Orleans. I couldn't have made it without you, Mom. So, are you ready to get on the road again?

I would like to thank my pastor, Paul Mitchell, for preaching those radical messages that I keep writing about in my novels. To my reviewers: Seana Reeves, Lucinda Greene, Marva Williams, Kelly Adams, Carla Green and Jacquelin Thomas, thanks for your kind words and feedback. My readers will be grateful for your diligence.

My editor, Joylynn Jossel and the whole crew at Urban Books/Kensington who do an awesome job with editing my books and designing my book covers. They make it so much easier for me to get out there and promote my books once they've been printed, and I just wanted to say that I appreciate it. I'd also like to send a shout-out to my friend and publicist, Rhonda Bogan, and my agent, Natasha Kern. A special thanks to you all.

Numerous book clubs hosted meetings and invited me to their meetings; I had tons of fun. I'm looking forward to reviewing *Latter Rain* with you also. In other words, invite me over. Come on, I don't eat that much.☺

Seriously though, I am so grateful to the thousands of people who pick up my books and read them from cover to cover. I truly hope the books did not just entertain you. My prayer is that you have been inspired to live a better life in Christ. For what could be better than to live in the midst of God's perfect will for your life?

The book is dedicated to my five beautiful nieces. Their names are listed here in alphabetical order:

Derricka, Diamond, Jonae', Kivonna and Taijah

May you know the peace that only a life lived for Christ can bring, in Jesus' name, I pray this prayer for all of you.

# Prologue

Isaac lay on his cot rubbing his chin. This was his final wake up. His last morning as a federally mandated, underpaid license plate maker. Most would have been elated. But Isaac needed time to think. Time to put together what his new life outside of prison would look like. So, as the morning bell shook the prison walls, and hundreds of men stood to be loosed from the cells that held them bound, Isaac continued to rub his chin and ponder. He stretched his well-toned chocolate body and exhaled. Isaac was in an uncomfortable place. He'd given his life to Jesus and meant every word of his declaration. But did he really have what it took to live for the Lord outside the confines of prison?

Two things Isaac wanted—no needed—more than the air he breathed were to walk upright before the One who claimed his soul, and to be forgiven by the one who had claimed his heart oh so many years ago. Sweet Nina Lewis, his baby's mama. He thought he was strong, until she taught him how to withstand the storms of life. Thought he had all the answers, until she taught him how to bow his knee, and wait on God to bring the answer.

The bell stopped ringing and his cell unlocked. In about an hour, he would be released. Time for him to teach Miss Nina Lewis a few things. Isaac made up his cot, and then got on his knees. Most of the inmates joked about Isaac's morning routine. But Isaac could find nothing routine about his relationship with Jesus.

"Oh, Father, here I am, the one you cleansed. Thank you for being so faithful. Thank you for loving me in spite of all the things I've done. You're great and mighty, Lord. Help me to walk upright before you—you are a holy God. And you require your servants to be holy. May my life bring you glory. May I never grieve the Holy Spirit you have placed in me."

For some odd reason, he looked at his hands. Hands that had caused mass destruction. Hands that had destroyed not-so-innocent lives. "This is my pledge to you, Lord. I will never use these hands to destroy your people again. In Jesus' name I pray. Amen."

After communing with his Savior, Isaac walked through the morning mechanically. Didn't even notice the plaster falling from the walls, or the scratchy soap as he showered and shaved. He said his final goodbyes without catching a whiff of the mixture of urine, humidity and sweat that clung to the air.

"You keep walking with Jesus," Pete, his old cellmate, told him.

T-bone strutted over to him. "Don't worry about the prison ministry. I'm in this joint for another year, at least. I'll hold it together."

Isaac picked up the Bible and an assortment of workbook material the chaplain had given him and handed it to T-bone. "You'll need this stuff."

He walked away. No looking back, no regrets. He'd served his time and did God's will while in prison. Time for a new chapter. He'd received letters from countless preachers over the last year. Many had heard about the revival going on in this place.

Isaac was grateful for all that God allowed him to do while in prison. But right now, his son, Donavan, and Nina were on his mind. He wasn't sure if Nina could let go of the past and accept him back into her life. But he would do anything to make that happen. He tried to convince her that he was different every time she brought his son for a visit. But Nina made it clear that she wasn't interested, and was only there to provide Donavan a ride home.

He picked up his two hundred dollar check for five years of service. Isaac owed a lot of back child support. How was he supposed to pay what he owed with two-hundred dollars? His hand tightened around the check. He wanted to ball it up and throw it in the guard's smug face, but that would go against his pledge to God. The prison doors opened. He felt like Mel Gibson in *Braveheart*, screaming FREEDOM!

He put the check in his pocket and walked out. Walking up the street toward the pick-up zone, the brisk March wind swirled around him. He zipped his jacket and stuffed his hands in his pockets, all the while hoping that Keith, his best friend for more than two decades would not be late. Entering the pick-up zone, Isaac spotted a broken down Ford Taurus, a red Lincoln Navigator with spinners and a black and gray Cadillac Seville. Keith was in none of them. The guy in the Navigator got out and headed over to him.

His smile showed off his gold plated mouth. His jeweled hands seemed out of place with his baggy Nike jogging suit.

"Isaac, my man. How's it going?" He offered his hand. "I've been out here over an hour waiting on you to pop that spot."

Isaac glanced at the outstretched hand, then sucked his teeth while sizing up the hustler in front of him.

The hustler conceded. He put his hand down, rubbing it on the side of his pants. "You don't remember me? I'm

Mickey." He put his hands in the air, indicating someone about chest level to where he now stood. "Remember little Mickey Jones? I worked for you on Williams Street."

Mickey had gotten taller. At six feet, he now stood eye to eye with Isaac. Isaac remembered him, but with recognition came a flood of memories. The Williams Street turf war was the source of Isaac's nightmares. The whole thing was wicked from the start. Isaac had been losing money on Williams Street. A quick investigation told him that a hustler named Ray-Ray had moved in on his turf. By the time the episode was over, Isaac had been shot, Valerie, one of his girls, and Ray-Ray were dead. The only good memory he had of that night was of Nina birthing his son.

"Yeah, Mickey, I remember you." They did the Black man's handshake. Isaac's head nodded in the direction of the Navigator. "I see you've come up in the world."

His gold teeth glistened as he smiled. "Well, you know, I couldn't be a runner forever. You taught me better than that."

"You can't stay in the game forever, Mickey. The game gets played out, one way or another."

Mickey shook his head. "Nobody ran them streets like you did. You ain't played out, Isaac. That's why I came to get you."

A silver Mercedes pulled up next to the Navigator.

Mickey continued. "I already got you a house." He handed Isaac the keys to the Navigator. "I bought it for you. You don't have to worry about a thing. Me and you, Isaac. We will own the city of Dayton."

Isaac looked at the keys and studied the jewels on Mickey's hands. "Looks like you already own Dayton."

Mickey lit up the friendly skies with his smile again. "Man, there's room enough for both of us. I started in this business because of you."

Isaac flinched. Life would be so sweet if only he didn't

have to think about how many dead men walking he had started in this business.

A suit stepped out of the Mercedes. Armani down to his shoes, with a Sunday-go-to-meeting hat on his self-assured head. He trotted his well-to-do self in Isaac's direction.

"Isaac Walker?"

Isaac turned toward Mr. Well-to-do, wondering if he was getting ready to be gifted with a Mercedes next. Isaac didn't know how much of this he could take.

"That's me," Isaac said and the man extended his hand.

Isaac glanced at it, but his hands still felt like resting at his side. There was something about shaking a man's hand. Isaac didn't take it lightly. Shaking a man's hand connected you with him. It said, "I agree with you." And Isaac wasn't agreeable all the time.

"I'm Bishop William Sumler. Your friend, Keith, asked me to come and pick you up."

Isaac shook his head. He had to work on his trust issues. He took Bishop Sumler's hand and shook it gladly. "I thought Keith was picking me up."

"He had some car trouble. I told him that I wanted to meet you in person anyway. So I made the trip for him."

Mickey got fidgety. Started looking around. "Look, Isaac, can we get going? I really don't want to hang around this place any longer than necessary."

Bishop Sumler eyed Mickey as he moved a little closer to Isaac. "Is this young man a friend of yours?"

"Yeah," Isaac told him. "Me and Mickey go way back. As a matter of fact," Isaac lifted the keys in his hand, "Mickey just brought me a car to roll out of here in."

Bishop Sumler's high yellow cheeks reddened. "So you don't need a ride?"

"That's not what I said." Isaac plopped the keys back in Mickey's hand and told him, "Thanks for the offer. But I'm a new man now. I can't go back to life as usual."

Bishop Sumler put a possessive hand on Isaac's shoulder. "God is pleased with you. Just keep looking to Him for answers."

"That's what I intend to do." Isaac smiled at Mickey. "Thanks for looking out for me. I'll catch up with you another time—shoot the breeze or something."

Mickey backed away. "Alright, man. But if you change your mind, you know where to find me."

"Didn't I always?"

Mickey gave a small, nervous laugh. "Yeah, I guess you did." He opened the door to his Navigator. "Well, keep holding it down. I'll see you on the other side."

"I sure hope so," Isaac said, even though he knew they were thinking of two different sides. Mickey wanted to see Isaac back on the gang-banging drug dealing side. While the side Isaac hoped to see Mickey on had pearly gates and streets of gold.

"You ready?" Bishop Sumler asked.

Isaac hesitated for a moment. Something in Mickey's eyes, in his nervous laughter, made Isaac uneasy. He wanted to catch up with him and tell him about life after the game. Let him know that there is a man named Jesus who could change his whole world in the blink of an eye. But he let it go. "Yeah, let's get out of here. I'm ready for something new."

# 1

*Five years later*

Nine long hours on the road had beaten him down. All Isaac wanted to do was grab hold of his pillow and power nap himself into the land of the unconscious. Opening the door to his two-bedroom roach motel never felt better. Actually, he didn't have roaches, but Isaac expected them any day now. Oh, how the mighty have fallen. If anyone had told him that accepting Jesus meant giving up everything and starting from scratch, he would have rebuked that devil. But here he was, suffering for Jesus.

Three steps into his apartment the floorboard creaked. Another five steps, creak. Two more steps, creak, creak. His slumlord promised to fix that months ago. Isaac pulled at his tie as he shook his head. "You can't trust nobody but Jesus."

Isaac set his mind to endure the lean years. He knew that once he was pastor of his own church, things would get better. Bishop Sumler had promised him that. So he'd moved to Chicago to work in the ministry at Bishop Sumler's church after getting out of prison. He'd been going from town to town with Bishop, learning the ropes of evangelism ever since.

On the road, he was king. Traveling with Bishop Sumler gave him privileges a young struggling preacher wouldn't have normally had. Bishop Sumler wasn't a Motel 6 kind of man. When a congregation put him up for the night, they had to dig deep in their pockets. And if meals were included, even Isaac, the armor bearer, had steak that night.

Unbuttoning his good as new, but-still-used-to-be-somebody-else's, Italian knit shirt, he stepped into his bedroom and flicked on the lights. He'd asked Cassandra to check on his apartment while he was away, to make sure the TV and DVD player stayed where he'd left them, and to water the one lonely plant that had bothered to stay alive in this dump. But he did not ask her to warm his bed.

"Cassandra!"

She jumped. The cover fell off her body as she stretched and yawned. "What took you so long?"

Had he given a nutcase the keys to his apartment? Something had to be wrong with her. She was in his bed, acting as if this was where she belonged. Talking 'bout, "What took you so long?" like they had been married for ten years and had five kids already.

"Um, Cassandra, can you tell me why you slept over?"

She wiped the sleep buggers from her big brown eyes, then looked at him as if to say, you know-what's-up. "I've been waiting for you, baby. Now, I know you're tired." She pulled the cover back as she scooted over.

His eyes feasted on her black silk, low cut negligee.

"Climb on in, baby. I warmed that spot just for you."

His mouth opened. No words escaped, but a little drool did swim down his chin. Wiping his unsanctified mouth and turning toward his bathroom, he told her, "I'll be right back."

He buttoned his shirt as he stepped into the bathroom. Looking to heaven he asked, "Lord, why have you allowed

this? How much temptation does one man have to endure?"
He fell to his knees, elbows touching the toilet seat lid,
hands entwined, head bowed. "Oh God, my Lord and my
King, You know that I am just a man. I can't handle this kind
of temptation, yet it keeps coming my way.

"You know me, Lord. I want to go out there, toss Cassandra up and repent later." He waited a minute to hear what
God would say to that. No answer came, but Isaac knew. He
was born to do God's will, even when it conflicted with his
own.

He stood, shook off the old man and slowly opened the
door. He hated feeling like a peeping Tom in his own house.
But there he was, door cocked open, peering out at the woman
sprawled across his bed. Lying on her stomach, the round-
ness of her backside was in full view. He closed the bathroom
door like a punk and fell back on his knees. "I can't do this,
Lord. How can you allow me to suffer like this?"

Isaac closed his eyes as his mind turned to Jesus, bruised
and beaten, hanging on a cross for the sins of the world. "I
am not worthy to suffer with you." He hung his head low.
"But if you could endure death by crucifixion, surely I can
crucify my body."

This time when he stood, his old nature was truly under
subjection. He opened the bathroom door with boldness.
"Cassandra, you've got to go."

Cassandra jumped as Isaac's words vibrated off the bedroom walls. "Wha . . . what's wrong?" She giggled nervously.
"It's still dark out, Isaac. I can't go now."

Isaac grabbed her ankle length skirt and turtleneck off the
dresser and threw them at her. "Get your clothes on, you
have got to go." She opened her mouth to protest. "I'm not
throwing out jokes, Cassandra. But I will throw you out, if
you're not dressed and gone in two minutes."

She rolled her eyes and got out of his bed. "Whatever,
man. You're the one missing out."

Isaac shook his head as he watched the praise leader at his church squeeze into her long conservative skirt. He thought Cassandra was different, but she was just like all the rest; trying to get in his pants. That thought almost made him burst out laughing. All his life he had been a sexual predator. But he was doing this thing for Jesus now. No room for compromise. Straight and narrow was the only walk his Lord would accept. He had slipped once. He vowed never to let it happen again.

"Denise said that you used to love for her to surprise you like this when you returned home." Cassandra put on her shoes and continued pouting. "What's wrong? You don't think I'd be as good as Denise?"

"Just give me my key and get out." She took his key off her key ring and threw it at him. Isaac sat on his bed, shoulders slumped, and allowed his heart to fill with shame as Cassandra slammed his door. How he'd gotten caught up again, Isaac didn't know. It had been two years since that thing with Denise. After confusing Denise so bad that she still didn't know it was wrong to fornicate, Isaac had sworn that he would never lie in bed with another woman that wasn't his wife. Every time he thought about how he'd messed up Denise's life, Isaac remembered Cynda Stevens.

For a time, Cynda's beauty outweighed the defects of her personality. Isaac had used her to make Nina jealous. But that had been years ago. He'd also passed Cynda on to his old friend, Spoony, when he was done with her. The guilt of that still ate at him. Spoony had turned Cynda out.

Isaac looked to heaven. "I thought you cast sins into this great sea and stop thinking about them." He sat in miserable silence as he waited on the Lord to soothe his soul. He was truly trying to change his life. He just didn't know why he kept finding himself in the same place. After five years of being out of prison and working in the ministry, Isaac still had so much anger in his heart. Sometimes he thought that his short lived affair with Denise was the cause of his stunted spiritual growth.

Eyes still lifted heavenward, Isaac asked the Lord, "When will I stop paying for the mistakes I've made?"

The room was silent again, then Isaac heard the voice of God say to him, *To whom much is given, much is required.*

He fell back on his bed and sighed. "I'm sorry, Lord. I never meant to hurt you. I'll get this thing right, if it's the last thing I do." He wanted to talk to his Lord a little while longer, plead his case. But his eyelids won the battle and sleep consumed his soul.

Dreams were much better than reality anyway, when Nina was the star of the show playing in his head, Isaac could sleep for days. She was wearing that hand-me-down blue jean dress that looked so good on her that she used to wear when she worked for him at his Laundromat. She walked toward him smiling. No, she didn't just walk. Baby-girl strutted with purpose. Confident of who she was and what she wanted. He always did like a woman who had her mind made up.

"It's time, Isaac," she told him with fire in her eyes.

He gave her an 'I got you now smile' as his dimples dipped into his chocolate coated face. "You ready for this?"

Her head bobbed.

He reached out for her, but it wasn't Nina anymore. His mother was now in front of him. She was falling. Oh, God! He couldn't catch her. Her head hit the table. The glass shattered and his sweet mother lay in a pool of blood.

"Nooooo!" Isaac bolted upright, panting, as sweat drizzled down his face. He ran his hands from his forehead to the back of his head.

Bam . . . bam . . . bam.

Before he could calm his nerves, Isaac realized that some lunatic was trying to knock his door down. The half moon that still clung to the sky told him that it was way too early for visitors. The sound would have normally irritated him and curled his fists. But right now, he was grateful for anything that would pull him out of bed.

He trodded through his bedroom and the creak, creak, creak of his living room. The bamming stopped once he stepped in the living room. He'd never be able to sneak up on a burglar in this mug. Rubbing his eyes with the palm of his hands, he looked through the peephole then flung open the door. "Man, it's five in the morning. What's the emergency?"

Keith stepped in, clothes wrinkled—hair hadn't seen a brush. "I've been trying to call you."

Isaac plucked a fur ball out of Keith's low-cut fade. "You must have been dialing the wrong number. I've been home since about two."

Keith picked up Isaac's phone and put the receiver to his ear. "No dial tone."

"What do you mean there's no dial tone?" He grabbed the phone to investigate. "Man, I know I paid this bill."

Keith raised his hands. "Calm down. Maybe something's wrong with your line." He walked away from Isaac. "Let me check the phone in your bedroom."

Isaac looked to heaven. "This suffering for Christ stuff is getting old."

"Here's the problem," Keith hollered from the bedroom. "You had the phone off the hook."

Isaac clenched his fist. "Cassandra must have done that. I'm so tired of these Holy Ghost filled jigga boos. I'm gon' have to get me a woman off the street. Maybe she'll respect the fact that I'm trying to live saved."

"Another one trying to give you the midnight special?"

Isaac shook his head. "I ain't gon' lie, Keith. I almost took it." Keith smiled, then his expression changed, like something was wrong. Real wrong. "What's up, man? Why you stalking me at this hour?"

Putting the phone back on the receiver, Keith sucked in his breath. "Sit down, Isaac."

"Just tell me what's up." Isaac got in his mac-daddy stance. "I can take it."

"I'm not joking, Isaac. I really think you should sit down for this."

Isaac folded his arms across his chest. "Look, I'm a man. I can take your news standing up."

Keith opened his mouth, then closed it. He stood there contemplating his options. He shook his head. Sometimes there was just no reasoning with Isaac. "There's been a shooting."

Isaac unfolded his arms. "Someone at the church?"

Keith shook his head.

Isaac hunched his shoulders. "Don't just stand there. Who got shot?"

Moisture creased the edges of Keith's eyes. "I-Isaac, can y-you please sit down?"

"Just spit it out."

"Someone drove by their house about one o'clock this morning. Nina must have been waiting up for Donavan. As soon as he stepped on the porch, she opened the door. The neighbors said she was yelling at him when the shooting started."

Isaac's knees buckled. "Are you trying to tell me that my family is dead?" Now his dream made sense. He'd seen Nina's face before he saw his mother lying in a pool of blood.

The moisture escaped Keith's eyes and ran down his cheeks. Isaac's legs gave out and he fell to his knees. "The last I heard they were in surgery."

"Oh, God; not my family." Isaac pulled at his shirt. Ripping it, just as his heart was being ripped.

Keith wiped his face with his shirtsleeve, then tried to pull Isaac up. Isaac yanked away from him. "Come on, man. Dayton is hours from here. We've got to get going."

Isaac didn't hear him. Couldn't hear anything from the turmoil going on in his head. For as long as he'd known Nina, his life had been about loving her and their son. A decade plus, hadn't changed that. Nina's unwillingness to come back to him hadn't changed that. And now some bullet was supposed to end the dreams he had for his family.

He looked toward heaven. "God, do what you want to me. I can take it. But not my family. Please don't destroy my family like this."

# 2

*Six weeks earlier*

The night air was cold and wet. Or was it hot and sticky? Nina Lewis rolled those thoughts around as her fingers tapped the keyboard. If anyone asked, she'd most likely admit that scene setting was the least favorite part of her job. She loved the telling of a good story. Loved to send her readers on a rollercoaster ride from page one to three hundred. But setting the stage to tell the story always gave her pause.

She rested her palms on her forehead, trying to sort out the scene. Her stories dealt with real people, real issues. Like Ramona, the heroine of her third book, trying to decide whether to have an abortion or trust that God was able to see her through single parenting. Or, Johnson Smalls, the ex-hustler/hero in her first and second books, struggling to live for the Lord in an ungodly world.

Her characters' lives, situations and circumstances were not always neatly packaged in a saved, sanctified, Holy Ghost filled, got-a-mind-to-run-on-and-see-what-the-end's-gon'-be body. But this is what she knew: the struggle of life, and God's great big ability to turn it all around for His glory. She was awed by the fact that He had chosen her to tell redemption's story. She didn't take this call on her life lightly. She prayed constantly, asking God for guidance. "What will this character do next? What's this scene about, Lord?"

God's guidance also gave her pause at times. Like now. Ramona had decided to keep the baby she was carrying. But she was struggling with the knowledge of the abortion she'd had a couple of years prior. Ramona wondered if God had forgiven her, or if she would still have to pay for the mistakes of her past.

God was speaking into Nina's spirit. Telling her that He casts sins into the sea and decides not to remember them. Nina stood and paced the length of the room. "Oh, God, help me to believe it."

This was Nina's greatest sin against God. Murder. After eleven years of living for the Lord, she still hadn't forgiven herself for the abortion she had as a teenager. So, how could she encourage her readers when she didn't fully believe?

Her hands plowed through her short, layered hair. "Why do you have me on this subject, Lord?"

Even as she asked the question she knew. The Lord had given her the same gentle answer when she first asked the question. *It's time.* Yes, Nina knew. The writing of this book was not just for her readers. This book would resurrect her demons. But could she slay them this time? Would she ever be free from this thing—this haunting?

If she didn't have enough problems, Donavan had plum lost his mind again. But that was to be expected. Every time Isaac used the work of the ministry as an excuse to neglect his son, Donavan started tripping. This time he had outdone himself. He was staying out way past an eleven-year-old's eight o'clock curfew. Hanging out with some older up-to-no-good thugs down at the neighborhood park. She'd caught him down there a couple of times and ran him home. His grades in school had gone from Bs and Cs to Ds and Fs. She'd gotten him a tutor and had shown up at the school unannounced to see what he was doing, since he obviously wasn't doing his school work. Each time she sat in one of his classes, Donavan would come home promising to do better. He'd beg her not to sit in his class again—he was losing cool points with his homies. But Nina didn't care about his cool points. Day by day she was losing her son, and she was determined to do something about it.

Up until six months ago, she had been working two jobs and writing in her spare time just to make ends meet. Then readers started spreading the word about her books. Bookstores started carrying more than just a few of her books at a time and church groups began ordering her books in bulk. Soon, she earned enough that she was able to quit both jobs and devote herself to Donavan and her writing career.

Nina had promised herself that as soon as her next royalty check came in, she would put her house up for sale and move her son into a better neighborhood.

That thought brought another problem to mind. Nina gnawed at her nail, agonizing over the fact that she and Donavan could be living in a much better neighborhood sooner, if she would just go on and plan her wedding.

She stood with fist clenched. "Oooh, if only Isaac hadn't filled Donavan's head with all his *we are family* crap." She wouldn't be so worried about telling Donavan that she was going to marry Charles Douglas III.

That's right. Love had finally come her way. And it was in the form of a fine, six-foot-two assistant district attorney with political aspirations. A man with principles, and no felonies. Instead of rejoicing over Charles's declaration of love, she had hidden his engagement ring in her jewelry box and asked him to be patient. How long did she expect him to wait? Was she crazy? Wasn't this what she had been waiting for all her life?

Thirty-six, but didn't look a day over twenty-seven. Thank you very much. Saved now eleven years. She had kept her vow to God, she wouldn't have even considered fornicating. But she was tired of waiting. She wanted her husband—and excuse the bluntness—the rumpled sheets that came with him.

Someone knocked on the door. Nina jumped. "Get yourself together, girl." She tugged and pulled at her sage green knit dress as she looked through the peephole. Charles was on her porch, peering at her, as she looked at him through the peephole. Nina smiled and stepped back, opening the door. His navy blue, I'm-a-businessman suit fit nicely on his three-nights-a-week-at-the-gym form. Being five-foot-three with heels on, Nina got a crick in her neck staring at such close proximity. But the man was so fine she didn't care. She stood her ground and took in the black mustache against that satin, caramel skin. The shine on his bald head was more provocative than a saved woman should dwell on.

Nina stepped back. "I didn't expect to see you this evening."

"I couldn't go home without bringing these to you." He pulled his hand from behind his back and showed off two dozen lilies.

She grabbed the flowers and hugged them to her chest. Lilies were her favorite flower. Charles strutted through her living room as Nina smelled her beautiful flowers. Nina's eyes moved from the lilies to study Charles. She couldn't help it. He had the walk of a man who knew who he was, and didn't care if the rest of the world ever figured it out. King Charles he would have been called, if he'd been born before they shackled and shipped us to the land of the free.

"Come sit over here with me, Nina."

She smiled. He liked to run the show. She didn't mind, much. She set her flowers on the dining room table and moved toward the love seat, where Charles sat, unbuttoning his jacket. "How was your day?" she asked, squeezing in next to him.

He sighed. "Things didn't go so well today. The Feds finally brought in this hustler I've wanted to prosecute for years. His preliminary hearing was today. I thought I had him when the judge gave him a million dollar bond, but he was back on the street by the end of the day."

Nina frowned. "Do you have enough evidence to get a verdict?"

"Without a doubt. That punk is into everything, but Jesus. The Feds have two hours worth of film showing Mickey Jones's drug dealing and the rest of his felonious activities. The boy even video taped himself as he counted his money and sold the drugs."

She rubbed his arm for support. "Well then, he may have won the battle, but you've got the war. Just leave it in God's hands."

He pulled her hand from his arm and covered it with both his hands. "That's why I had to see you today. You know how to make me feel better."

Smiling felt good. A long time coming was this man.

He patted and rubbed her hand. "I didn't come over here to talk about that low-life."

Nina flinched. Yeah, this Mickey Jones was a drug dealer, and maybe he should be put in jail, but did that mean he was too low for God to redeem?

"I know what you're thinking, Nina. Yes, I'm sure that God can deliver him. But you don't know everything he's done. Scum like this guy should be sent straight to the devil."

She kept silent.

He rubbed her finger; the one his ring should be on. She caught a glimpse of his dark eyes. Sad eyes. "I want to see it on your finger, Nina."

She tried to pull her hand away. He pulled it back. "I know, Charles. Be patient with me."

"How patient, baby?"

Nina opened her mouth to respond, but caught a glimpse of the door opening.

Before she could move, Donavan rushed in, accusing them. "What are you doing? Get your hands off my mother."

Nina pulled her hand from Charles's grip and stood. She saw the look of rejection on her fiancé's face and wanted to kick herself. She'd done it again—chosen Donavan over Charles. If this man was to be her husband, how could she continue justifying her actions?

# 3

Isaac and Keith sat in their small office counting the church offering and reviewing bills. The irony made Isaac laugh.

He and Keith used to count money in the crack houses he'd littered throughout the city of Dayton. At that time, Isaac's only concern was fattening his pockets. Money was power, and Isaac had more than his share of both.

"So what are you doing this weekend?" Keith asked while opening the last bill.

Isaac smiled. "Picking up Donavan. I had to cancel last weekend, so Nina agreed to switch off with me." He glanced at the imitation gold plated watch on his wrist. It was three o'clock. He was supposed to be there by now. Nina was going to kill him.

Keith whistled.

"What's up?" Isaac asked.

"Man, didn't we already purchase all the lumber MacMillan needed?"

"Last month. Why?"

Keith handed Isaac the latest bill from MacMillan Construction. "Looks like we're getting fleeced."

*Fleeced indeed,* Isaac thought as he looked at the twenty thousand dollar bill for items that had already been bought and paid for. "This dude must think he's dealing with some suckas."

"Who is stupid enough to take the two of you for suckers?"

Isaac turned to greet Bishop Sumler as he strutted into their world. He had his priestly collar on with gray pinstriped pants and a jacket to match, with a black vest.

"Hey, Bishop," Isaac said.

"Hey, yourself. I know that look on your face." Bishop's eyebrow arched as he asked, "What's wrong, Isaac?"

Isaac handed over the bill. Bishop Sumler reviewed it and frowned. "I thought we already paid for the lumber."

"Exactly," Keith responded.

"And what's this overtime charge? Every time I drive by the site, MacMillan's workers are on break." Bishop shook his head. "I need to call our lawyers so they can look into this."

Isaac clenched his fists. "Where I come from, a two-by-four up side MacMillan's fat head would have 'paid-in-full' stamped on this bill before we wasted a dime on a lawyer."

Bishop laughed. "That would certainly get results. But I don't think we want to be the feature story on the evening news, now do we?"

Actually, it had been a while since Isaac had been on the news. He wouldn't mind a little drama about now. Something to spice things up a bit.

Keith shrugged and folded his hands in his lap. "What do you want to do about this, Bishop?"

Sometimes Keith's mouth fixed on the stupidest questions. "What do you think?" Isaac boomed. "We need to go down there and take care of this."

"Good." Bishop patted Isaac on the back. "You boys go handle this. But just talk to the man. Try not to let your temper flare, Isaac."

Easier said than done, especially when Isaac was already hot.

Bishop began to walk out, then snapped his fingers as he turned back to Isaac. "Almost forgot what I came to see you about. Can you deliver the sermon on Sunday?"

Isaac was going to have Donavan this weekend. Would he have time to prepare a sermon? He looked at his watch. Already an hour late picking up his son and he still had MacMillan and five hours of road time in his way. "This is probably not the best weekend for me, sir."

"I know this is short notice, Isaac, but I'm going to be out of town. I really need your help."

Since he'd been an armor bearer for Bishop, he'd only preached about three times. Bishop didn't like to share his pulpit. Naturally, Isaac was honored that Bishop would share it with him. "I'll make it work. It's not a problem."

Bishop smiled. "That's good. That's good. Oh, and Cassandra Davis will be visiting our church this Sunday. She's trying to decide whether to join our church or Bishop Marks's."

Isaac was silent.

A devilish grin eked out before Bishop could control himself. "I told her you would take her out to dinner after church."

The phone rang. Keith picked it up.

All the mess Isaac had gone through with Denise Wilkerson was because of Bishop Sumler's match making. After Denise, there was Stacey, the tongue talking, Holy Ghost filled stripper. Then Therese, the fire baptized got-a-mind-to-run-on-and-sleep-with-all-the-preachers woman. Isaac was beginning to wonder if Bishop could even recognize a saved woman from all the imitation saints he kept trying to hook him up with.

Keith held the phone out to Isaac. "It's Nina."

Isaac grabbed the phone, but before putting the receiver to his ear, he told Bishop, "I don't know about dinner on Sunday."

"Well, at least meet with her after church. She would make an excellent praise leader, and you know we've been needing a praise leader since Stacey left."

Oh, so now it was his fault that Stacey the stripper kept trying to get with him. The moment he told her he didn't want her free-will offering, she changed membership. Good riddance, and God help her new pastor. "I'll think about it," he told Bishop as he put the receiver to his ear. "Hey you."

No hello, or how you doing. Nothing. She just got straight to the point. "Why aren't you here?"

Bishop Sumler put the bill back on his desk and walked out.

Isaac hesitated, then sat down. "Um, I got caught up."

Smirking, she said, "Mmph, I know what that means."

"Why are you always judging me? You don't know what I'm doing."

"I know that you're still in Chicago. And I know that your son will be walking in this house within five minutes wondering why he wasn't important enough for his father to spend some time with him."

Isaac looked at the papers on his desk. The MacMillan Construction bill glared at him, daring him to leave town without handling his business. "Look, Nina, I'm on my way. I just need to take care of something first. Can you tell Donavan to wait for me?"

"Like last time?"

Isaac closed his eyes and ran his hand through his wavy hair. This woman could use a refresher course on forgiving and forgetting. "I'm coming, Nina. Trust me on that."

Isaac felt the heat of the silence that spoke volumes from Nina's end.

"I'll be there around eight-thirty, nine o'clock. Okay, Nina?"

"Don't worry about it, Isaac. I think I know how to solve this problem." She hung up.

Isaac slammed the phone down. "She's always on me about something. You'd think I was a dead-beat looking for a way out of child support."

"Let it go. Nina is probably just frustrated right now," Keith told him.

"She's trippin' on something." He picked up his keys. "Look, let's just go take care of our issue with MacMillan so I can get on the road."

As they drove down the street, headed toward the construction site, Keith laughed. "Man, Bishop is gon' make sure you jump the broom."

Isaac shook his head. "Sometimes I wonder."

Keith stopped laughing and looked at his friend. "What's wrong?"

Isaac scratched the itch at the top of his head. "Well, if he wants me married so bad, why does he keep hooking me up with these free-will-love-offering sisters?"

"I've wondered that myself. I don't think Bishop would know a good woman if she fell on him."

Isaac pulled the car up to the construction site. "I wish he would introduce me to someone like Nina." He turned off the car. "Man, who am I kidding? I wish I had Nina."

"I know how you feel," Keith said as his eyes saddened and he turned away from his friend. If the truth was told, Keith wished that he had met Nina first.

"That's my family." Isaac pounded the steering wheel with his fist. "If only Nina would just let go of the past and see the truth."

Keith was silent. Then, after mulling it over, he turned to

Isaac. "You're right, man. Nina and Donavan are your family. So, be there for them."

Isaac turned his gaze toward the construction site and sneered, "Look at him. Charging us for overtime while his crew sits on their butts." They got out of the car and walked past the workers as they sat around waiting for day to break so they could start collecting overtime. One of the workers stood and stretched. He'd obviously had more than his share of stuffed pizza and Italian sausages.

Isaac stopped and did a double take. Besides, there was something hauntingly familiar about this man. One piercing glance later and Isaac knew. Their eyes locked. A rage boiled in Isaac. He reached toward his back for his Glock. Then he remembered that saying yes to Jesus meant giving up his weapons of mass destruction. Ah, salvation did have its limitations.

He wasn't beaten yet, though. He stalked over to MacMillan and demanded. "What's he doing here?"

MacMillan glanced in the direction of Isaac's pointer finger. "Who, Marvin? He works for me."

"Not on this site, he doesn't. I want him gone today!"

"Come on, man. He's one of my best workers." MacMillan saw the unyielding look in Isaac's eyes and quietly added, "He's got a family."

Isaac sucked his teeth and stared him down.

Keith turned toward Marvin. All the workers could hear what Isaac was saying. Marvin's eyes were downcast. He bent down to pick up his lunch box and grabbed his jacket. There was something familiar about the man that Keith couldn't put his finger on.

Marvin shook a couple of his team members' hands and turned to walk off the site. MacMillan hollered after him. "Marvin, don't go. You don't have to leave."

Marvin held up a hand, but kept walking.

"Let him go," Isaac told MacMillan.

Keith continued to watch Marvin. Even while being thrown off a job site, his walk was full of confidence and brass. A man with a walk like that was too stubborn to back down, even if the world was against him. But he had backed down, hadn't he?

MacMillan's hands flayed in the air. "Well, this is outrageous! Just outrageous."

"No. This is outrageous." Isaac took the paper out of his pocket and handed it to MacMillan.

"It's your bill." He shrugged. "What's wrong with it?"

Isaac pointed at a section of the bill. "Now, I'm not as educated as you are, so I'm going to need you to explain why we need to pay for lumber twice?"

MacMillan stammered, "Y-you're not paying twice. We had to order more lumber. This job is going to be bigger than we estimated."

Isaac's lip curled. "Mmph." He pointed at another section of the bill. "How you gon' charge us overtime, when your men sit out here on break half the day?"

"Come on, man. I'm doing this job for half the cost. How could you not trust me?"

Isaac smirked as he told MacMillan, "I don't trust nobody but Jesus."

MacMillan rubbed his temples. His eyes rolled upward. "Look, Isaac. The bill is legit. Now you guys can either pay it, or I'll stop construction on this church right now."

"What did you just say to me?"

MacMillan puffed out his chest. "I said that I'll stop construction if you don't pay your bill."

The eyes of a predator blazed fury as Isaac grabbed a fist full of MacMillan's collar. "I'm going to do you a favor and give you a second chance." He smashed the bill in MacMillan's face. "Fleecing me is not good for your health. You sure you want to do that?"

Keith's hands went up to slow Isaac's madness. "Man, what are you doing?"

"I'm gon' knock some sense into his thieving head."

Keith stuttered "C-come on, I-Isaac. This ain't w-what we came down here to do."

Isaac tightened his grip. "We didn't come down here to get robbed either. I'm gon' bust his head open, then we'll see if he still thinks this bill is legit."

MacMillan caught Keith's stuttering disease. "N-now, I-if you hit me. I-I'm going to call the p-p-police."

Isaac smirked again. "You'll have to get to the phone to do that."

"Come on, man. There's a better way," Keith said.

"Shut up, Keith. The non-violence movement died when they shot Martin Luther King, Jr." Isaac glared at MacMillan. "When I get through beating you down, you won't have the strength to cheat another custom—"

"Help! Help me," MacMillan screamed.

A couple of MacMillan's men stood up and weighed their options.

Isaac told MacMillan, "You'll be in a coma before they get me off you."

MacMillan struggled to free himself from Isaac's death grip. "Okay, okay. Let me look at the bill again."

Isaac loosed him, picked the bill off the ground and handed it to MacMillan.

A nervous laugh escaped MacMillan's thin lips as he studied the bill. "Hey, you gentlemen might be right." He snapped his finger. "Now that I think about it, you guys paid for your lumber about three months ago. I'm going to have the accounting department go over this bill one more time."

Neither Keith nor Isaac responded. Just stared him down.

"Come on, fellows. I'm human, I make mistakes. Aren't you people supposed to forgive and forget?"

"Yeah, I'll forgive you when you stop cheating us. But, I

haven't forgotten nothing since I was three years old, and you better believe I'll remember this mess." Isaac turned and walked toward the car. His shoulders slumped with the weight of memories.

Keith stood back and watched him. Then he saw it. Isaac walked with confidence and brass.

# 4

Nina and Charles held a unified front as Donavan glared at them. The afternoon sun shone through her picture window and danced on the engagement ring on her finger. It shimmered. She smiled. Was it so wrong that she should be happy? Nina had finally put the ring on after Donavan walked in the house and demanded that Charles leave her alone. She told Donavan that she was engaged and showed him the proof of her engagement.

"I don't believe you!" Donavan roared. "How can you do this to our family?"

"I'm not doing anything to our family. I'm doing this *for* our family, Donavan."

All her life, Nina wanted to have a family; a unit that would be there, no matter what. Couldn't Donavan understand that? She was just trying to give him something she didn't have growing up. Nina's birth mother gave her up for adoption when she was four years old. The only thing she remembered about the woman was their goodbye.

Standing in front of an orphanage her mother told her, "I love you, Nina. That's why I'm doing this."

To this day, Nina still wondered how someone could love her and give her away at the same time. Her adoptive parents were good to her, but they died in a car wreck when she was in high school.

Donavan laughed and turned to Charles. "I suppose you think my dad is going to fall all over himself thanking you for what you're doing to his family?"

"Donavan!" Nina wondered why Isaac had to fill his head with impossible dreams; things that would never come to pass. "You and I are a family; that's it. And Charles wants to be a part of our family. You're going to have to face the fact that I'm not going to marry your dad."

Donavan's throat constricted as his eyes narrowed. He had his father's eyes. Dark and dangerous. "Why do you have to ruin everything?"

Charles stood and put his hand on Donavan's shoulder. "We're not trying to ruin anything for you, son."

"I'm not your son. I've got a daddy," Donavan told him while rolling his eyes.

Charles lifted his hands in surrender. "You're right, Donavan. You already have a father. But I love your mom and she has agreed to marry me—we want to be a family."

Nina noticed that Charles did not tell Donavan that she loved him. Did he have doubts about her love? She smiled at her future husband, trying to portray the love her lips hadn't been able to say.

"Where's my dad? He should have been here by now."

*Your no-good daddy is too busy to leave Chicago for someone as unimportant as his son.* That's what she wanted to say. Putting her thoughts in check, she told him, "I'm not sure if your dad will be able to make it."

Donavan fought a good fight, but his eyes misted anyway. "Oh, so I guess this is the," he mimicked Nina's soft, patient voice, "Cheer up, Donavan. Your dad is a loser, but I've got a new daddy for you, talk. Is that it?"

Charles was in his "I object" courtroom stance. His hands gripped the sofa. "We are not going to tolerate your disrespect, young man."

"You don't have to tolerate nothing from me. I don't need you. I didn't ask to be born," Donavan said as he stormed out of the house.

Isaac always left her to deal with his mess. Oooh, he infuriated her. Made her want to bring her lunch back up. Nina got up and followed her son. "You get back here right now."

Donavan pushed his bike off the porch and sped off.

"Donavan! Donavan, get back here," Nina hollered as she watched her son continue riding his bike down the street.

Charles walked onto the porch. Nina kept screaming for her son.

"Come on back inside, baby," Charles told her while shaking his head in frustration.

"No!" She rushed down the stairs. "Donavan, don't do this! Turn that bike around this minute." Donavan kept going. She stood there until he was out of sight, wondering when she had lost control of her precious son.

Life had not been easy for her and Donavan. After Isaac went to jail, she worked two and three jobs just to make ends meet. And then there was college. She thought the time she spent away from Donavan would be worth it once she graduated from college and was able to provide for him. But here she was, making a decent enough living as a writer with time to spend with her son, and he was moving farther and farther away from her.

"Come on, baby." Charles pulled at her. "Let's go back inside."

Nina turned toward Charles.

Seeing the desperate look in her eyes, he grabbed her and hugged her close. "He'll be back—just needs to cool down some, that's all."

* * *

Across the street, Mickey Jones sat in a black Maxima with tinted windows. He smiled as he watched Charles cling to his lady. "Lookie here, lookie here. The DA is in love."

This was going to be more interesting than Mickey imagined. His first thought was to kill the assistant district attorney. Charles had been on his back for years. Always hassling him, trying to get him locked down. He was worse than a gold digging stalker, blowing up his pager and cell phone. His nemesis was riding high now, thinking he had won. But Mickey hadn't begun to show him the meaning of loss. Oh, but Mr. Charles Douglas III would soon feel the wrath of the underworld. He would live to regret the day he decided to tangle with Mickey Jones.

The voices inside his head were screaming at him. They weren't very nice. "Loser—fake—you're a nothing—zero."

He shoved his hands against his ears. He wasn't a loser. He was top dog. Even Isaac had said so. What was it he had said? He moved his hand in the air as his fingers danced over the words, "*Looks like you already own Dayton.*" Yes, Isaac had been impressed with the way he had come up in the world. He hadn't accepted the car or the house Mickey had bought for him; a kind of get-out-of-jail present. But Mickey understood. Isaac was a preacher man now. But, oh, how he had dreamed of sharing his kingdom with Isaac. He was the only one he would share anything with. Not these other thugs in the street. He had a bullet waiting for each one of them. And he certainly wasn't sharing anything with these rotten voices he couldn't get rid of. Disrespecting him.

He rolled down his window, listening to Charles and his lady friend.

The assistant DA pulled his lady close to him. "Come on, Nina, let's go back inside."

She was crying. "Charles, I've got to go find him."

"Donavan will be back. He just needs to blow off a little steam. Trust me on this, baby. We'll work through this."

Nina looked skeptical.

Charles gave her an I-think-I-can, I-think-I-can look. "Oh, I'm up for the challenge. By the time we're married, I'll have Donavan wrapped around my finger. I'm telling you, Nina, we're going to be happy."

Mickey smirked. "Good luck with that," he said, while running his trigger finger along the barrel of his gun.

# 5

Donavan rode his bike to the park a couple of blocks from his house. He leaned his bike against a rusty, old, green trashcan and headed for the basketball court. A little one-on-one was what he needed. Something to take his mind off his family.

The court was full of overgrown brothers shooting hoops at four o'clock in the afternoon. God hadn't been able to convince these thugs that a man who doesn't work shouldn't eat. When they wanted food they got it with a gun and a ski mask. Donavan shook his head and wondered, yet again, what kind of person grows up with an allergic reaction to work. He'd asked as much to JC, the almost seven foot ex-NBA hopeful who was dominating the court right now. During his high school, eleven o'clock news making days, several universities offered him scholarships. One offered fifty thousand in cash. JC was packed and ready to flee the hood. He was going to take his game further than LeBron or Jordan ever did. But then that racist university asked him to take a drug test. To this day, JC spouts off about the unjust drug laws. If marijuana was a drug, then JC's mama was the

Queen of Egypt and they lived in a palace instead of the maggot infested dwelling that disgusted the roaches so bad, they packed up and moved to their less trifling next-door neighbors.

When JC wasn't complaining about the unjust drug laws, he was borrowing money and shaking down shorties like himself. Donavan had gone without lunch for a week the first time JC shook him. He was so mad he didn't care that he was a shortie and JC was next to a giant, he screamed at him, "Man, why don't you get a job?"

"Please. A job don't do nothing but keep you just-over-broke," JC had reasoned.

"Well, at least you won't be just-over-borrowing," Donavan countered.

JC laughed as he playfully shoved Donavan. "I like you, shortie. You're all right."

From that day on, JC became Donavan's protector; watching out for him throughout the neighborhood. There was an eight-year difference in their ages, but they were friends. It wasn't the Big Brother program Donovan's mama would have signed up for, but it worked.

JC saw Donavan standing at the edge of the court and waved as he checked his opponent.

Donavan lifted his chin to say, "What up?"

None of his school friends were balling, only the older guys. Donavan wasn't big enough to take any of them on yet. So he sat down and watched JC whup on a couple other unemployables. He put his foot on the basketball that was on the ground next to the bench he sat on. Put his hand under his chin, and sulked. If he wasn't so young maybe he could do some things to earn money and get out from under his mother's love-sick roof. His parents didn't have time for him. He was one big inconvenience they fit in around their busy ministries. His mom claimed that she left her day job to spend more time with him and focus on her writing. It was more like she left her job to focus on her writing and then spend time with him if she had the time. And with Charles always sniffing around, she rarely had exclusive time for him anymore.

As for his missing in action daddy, please. Every time he thought about Mister-I-love-Jesus-so-I'm-going-to-travel-the-world-preaching-the-Gospel-and-forget-all-about-the-son-I'm-suppose-to-help-raise, he got ill. Forget 'em. He didn't need mommy dearest or the rolling stone. If he ran away, it would probably take them a couple of days to miss him. No rumpled sheets. No dirty socks in the hallway. No milk left on the counter. Oh . . . Donavan must not be home.

"What's got your brows all scrunched up?"

Donavan looked up to see JC's sweat-drenched body standing before him. "What's up, man?"

"Nothing much." JC wiped the sweat from his face with the bottom of his tee-shirt and sat down. "What you doing here? Thought you was hanging out with your dad this weekend."

Donavan smirked. "Me too. But you know how that goes."

JC took Donavan's ball and bounced it. "Naw, Shortie, I don't know nothing about that. My old man ain't never stopped by to pick me up for no weekend visit. Shoot, when he ain't vacationing behind steel and concrete, I gotta drive by the winos on Fifth Street just to get a whiff of him."

# 6

"Nina, baby, come sit down."

She turned from the window, pulled back the curtains and shook her head as Charles patted the seat next to him. "I've got to go find Donavan."

Charles got up and walked over to where Nina stood peering out the front window. "Baby, don't do this to yourself." He pulled her away from the window and into his arms.

Tears filled Nina's eyes as she allowed Charles to hold her. "What am I supposed to do? I feel like a failure."

They sat on the couch. Charles rubbed her back and placed a kiss on her forehead. "You did the best you could, baby."

Her shoulders shook from the torrent of her tears. "B-but, h-he's been so hateful lately."

"You can't do this alone. When we're married, I'll become more active in Donavan's life." He wiped her tear soaked face and kissed her soft, wet lips. "Anyway, we'll have plenty of our own children. And they'll have a mother and father in the home right from the start."

Nina pulled herself from Charles's embrace and eyed him. "How many is plenty?"

He smiled. "Well, I figure that since you're already thirty-six, you can't have very many baby making years left."

Hands on hips, she challenged with an, "Excuse me?"

His hands went up in surrender. "I'm not saying that you're old. But realistically, baby, the clock is ticking."

She stood, mouth open. "I know you're not talking. I mean, you're thirty-nine."

He grabbed Nina and pulled her back on the couch next to him. Her back was pressed against his chest as he held her. "You know that men can have babies at just about any age. I could be a hundred years old and still impregnate a woman."

Nina's eyes got big. "You sound like you're trying to be like Abraham. That's all well and good for you, but I hope you're not looking for a Sarah; I'm not signing up for that job."

Charles laughed. He then rubbed Nina's shoulder and asked, "What do you think about having three more children?"

"I don't know." Nina said with a sigh. "My biological clock might blow up after the first child."

He laughed again. "You got me on that one." He turned her around to face him. "But, all jokes aside. I come from a big family. My mom had ten children. I always thought I'd have at least six or seven. But I'm willing to settle for three. What do you say?"

Nina always wanted more children. But it took so long for her knight in shining armor to show up, she'd given up on her dream. Donavan would be graduating from high school in about six years—setting off on his own soon after that. She could see herself writing more, traveling, and just enjoying life. But as she looked into Charles's eyes, she knew that this was something he needed. Who was she to deny him? "We'll give it our best shot."

# 7

Driving down Broadway, Isaac's heart sank. He had once ruled this area. He remembered stepping onto the grounds right across from Church's Chicken, on the corner of Broadway and Riverview, and claiming the land. Kinda like the gold rush days of old, but his pot of gold was crack. The Promised Land is what he had dubbed this area. His kingdom, and everybody in it, bowed down to him. Oh, how wrong he had been. He hated driving down these streets now. He wished Nina would move. Wished he didn't have to remember it all as if it were yesterday. Maybe that's why he got busy and didn't show up sometimes. He didn't do it on purpose. But these streets wouldn't let him forget. Even the graffiti still called out his name.

Every time he passed the alley that he set Mickey up in years ago, he thought of the lost look on Mickey's face the day Isaac got out of prison. For years now, Isaac had wondered if he'd made the right decision when he got into Bishop Sumler's car and left Mickey at the pick-up zone. Should he have left with Mickey? Would he have been able to convince him to give up the gangster life and accept Jesus?

Turning onto Oxford, he saw Nina sitting on the front porch. He knew right away that things weren't going to go well for him. Her arms were crossed tightly around her body, lip twisted, as she recognized his car. Even without being in close proximity, he could tell Nina had been crying.

Putt-putting his way into the parking spot in front of her house, his classic Oldsmobile passed gas as he shut off the engine. He got out of the car and fanned the air. He needed to get a new car, because this one was on its way to car heaven.

"Hey, you." He waved at the evil looking woman on the porch. Her arms continued to hug her body. Those sweet hazel eyes murdered him a thousand times. Summer was a month away, but it was chilly on this street.

Lately, all he got from Nina was harsh words and daggered eyes. Sometimes he wondered why he even bothered with the small talk. She had given him more respect when he was slapping her around. Maybe she missed getting beat down. Maybe she wanted him to man handle her. Then he stopped himself. *Wrong thinking. Really wrong thinking.* If he wanted respect, he was just gonna have to earn it. He lifted his hands in surrender, stepping onto the porch. "Whoa, bring it down a notch. I come in peace."

She stood and unfolded her arms. "What do you want, Isaac?"

"What do you mean, *what do I want*? I'm here to pick up Donavan." Despite himself, his eyes rolled upward. "We talked on the phone just a couple hours ago, remember?"

"Six hours ago, Isaac." Her voice rose and was a little shaky as she continued. "Not a couple hours ago. You should have been here by five. It's nine o'clock, and my son is not here."

"Where is he?"

"I don't know. He ran off."

"Didn't you tell him I was coming?" He was getting angry and sick of Nina's mess. "Why would you let my son run off when you knew I was on my way?"

"First of all," Nina shook her finger in his face, "I didn't let *your son* do anything. He's got a mind of his own. And we both know where he got that from."

Isaac started to open his mouth to defend himself, but Nina wasn't finished.

"And furthermore, how was I supposed to know you were on your way? You've cancelled on *your son* the last three times you were supposed to pick him up."

The truth of that statement calmed him. "Okay, Nina. I'm not here to argue with you. Just tell me where I can find Donavan."

She screamed, blowing salsa, chips and that chicken burrito she had for dinner in his face. "I don't know where he is. I told you he ran off." A tear trickled down her face. She sucked in her breath and put her hand over her mouth. "I can't believe he did this."

He touched the hand that held her mouth. The left one. The one that held that big rock. His mouth opened, then closed. He touched the diamonds encased in her ring.

Donavan picked that moment to roll his two-wheeler in front of the house, jump off and stomp up the stairs. "Well, look who's here," he said as he passed his father.

Isaac's eyes lingered on Nina and that—that ring, as he grabbed Donavan's shirttail and pulled him around. "Boy, where do you think you're going?"

Donavan puffed up. "In the house. Now let me go."

Slapping the backside of Donavan's head, Isaac told him, "It's nine o'clock at night. Where does your eleven-year-old half grown self get the nerve to roam the streets at night?"

Donavan jerked away from his father. "I can do what I want."

Isaac hit him again. "You can get beat down, is what you can do."

Nina raised her hand. "Stop hitting him, Isaac."

"The boy needs a good beating." He turned back to Donavan and shook him. "Isn't that right, Donny Boy? If I beat the snot out of you, the next time I ask you where you've been, you'll open that smart mouth and tell me real quick, won't 'cha?"

Donavan was silent.

Isaac raised his hand and eyed his son. "I asked you a question."

"Yes, sir. I-I was at the park."

Nina pulled Donavan away from Isaac. "Look at you. All you know is violence. Your father beat you all the time. Did it do you any good?"

Seeing red, Isaac turned away from Nina and glared at Donavan as he eased out of his hold. "Hey, go get your clothes, boy. And get back down here." Donavan scurried away, then Isaac turned back to Nina. "I told you not to mention that man to me. He was no father. He killed my mother, and you dare compare me to that man?"

"That's your problem, Isaac. You don't know how to let things go."

"Like you let us go?"

"What are you talking about? I didn't let anything go."

Isaac pointed at her engagement ring. "So, I guess that guy you've been seeing asked you to marry him?"

Lifting her hand and gazing at her ring she told Isaac, "It's about time Donavan had a mother and father in the same house. Don't you think?"

Isaac's lip curled as if he'd had a little too much mad cow. "I tried to give him that, but you didn't want me."

"No. I asked you to deal with your issues before coming to my doorstep. You refused to do it."

The way he'd remembered it was that he showed up on

her doorstep with hat in hand and begged her to marry him so that she and Donavan could move to Chicago with him. But all she wanted to talk about was his usually wrong daddy. Nina told him that he needed to find his father and set things right with him before she could even consider marrying him.

She acted like Isaac had the problem. Like he was supposed to go and thank his usually wrong daddy for smacking his mother around. Maybe he should treat him to dinner. Sit down over a few steaks and tell Usually Wrong how he felt when he saw his mother laid out in a pool of blood.

He'd only been thirteen when that monster took his sweet mother away from him and his brother. Donavan, his brother, was twelve and too young to die. But that didn't stop that bullet from exploding in his head while Isaac was in Juvee for beating Usually Wrong down. Maybe he should tell the old man that Donavan now resides in hell. But what would he care? And what did Nina know? Her save-the-world attitude really ticked him off sometimes. "Have it your way, Nina. Ruin your life with this guy. I'm tired of trying to live up to your high standards." He turned and stomped off the porch.

Before he reached the last step, Nina grabbed his arm and turned him back to face her. "Don't you pin this on me. You had your chance. If you really wanted us to be a family, you should have found your father so you could address your issues. But, no. You chose to follow behind that jack leg bishop and move to Chicago."

He pulled his arm from her grasp. "I'm not following behind nobody but God. And how do you know I haven't found my father?"

Nina's face lit up. Those hazel eyes sparkled, sparkled for him.

"Please tell me you mean it. When did you find him?"

"See how happy you are?" Isaac smirked. "And I know

why. You think that if I go to that old man and forgive him, then whatever demons I'm dealing with will be gone, and we'll be free to marry."

"Don't flatter yourself, Isaac," Nina told him while waving her ring finger in his face. "I'm already spoken for."

"Nina, are you really sure you want to marry that DA sucka?"

She folded her arms around her small frame once more. "I smiled because I want you to be happy, Isaac. Don't read more into it than there is."

"Whatever helps you put on that dress and walk down the aisle," he told her while opening his car door.

Before he could get in the car, Nina yelled after him. "Did you find your father or not, Isaac?"

Just before he slammed his car door and sped off he told her, "I saw him."

"Be a man, Isaac. Handle your business," she yelled at him.

# 8

Donavan was in his room angrily throwing clothes into his Cincinnati Reds duffle bag when he heard his father's car door slam. He walked over to the window just in time to see father of the year speed off like he was a carjacker running from the po-po. "That's right, Dad, get mad at her and forget that you even have a son. Leave me behind like you always do."

Donavan walked back over to his bed, picked up his duffle bag and poured the contents on the floor. He sat down, shoulders slumped, staring blankly at the wall. He tried to imagine what it would feel like if he mattered to somebody.

One day he would know what it felt like, and he wouldn't be part of no package deal either. His dad had this lovesick thing going on that said, if Nina Lewis wouldn't be his woman, then he needed directions to the nearest how-to-be-a-daddy boot camp.

Forget 'em. Donavan would make his own way in this world. As a matter of fact, he was going to find JC and see if he could hook him up with something. Only problem with going to JC was that JC would want to run his big mouth to Donavan's daddy. JC idolized Isaac.

"Man, your daddy was the Pope around here. Didn't nobody mess with the Ike-man. Not unless they wanted some instant death," JC had told him. Donavan didn't know the Ike-man JC drooled over. But if JC really wanted to know the truth, the Ike-man thought JC was a loser, and had told Donavan not to hang with him.

To Donavan, his daddy was the preaching man who must not have read the part in the Bible that said *a man who doesn't take care of his family is worse than an infidel.*

He opened his window. There was a knock at his door.

"Yeah?"

Without opening his bedroom door, Nina asked Donavan, "You want to pop some popcorn and watch a movie with me?"

With one foot out the window, he told her, "Naw, I'm cool."

She wasn't gone yet, he knew she was still standing on the other side of his door.

With her forehead pressed against his door and a tear running down her face, Nina said, "I'm sorry, Donavan."

"Don't sweat it, Mom. I'm all right."

He would show them. If the Ike-man had been the Pope, then he would become king. He had a self-assured smile on his face as he climbed out of the window. It still amazed him that his mom hadn't noticed that he had sneaked out of the house the last three Friday nights. But hey, when her life is so busy, busy, busy, who could expect her to add supervision of a wayward son to her to-do list?

Mickey sat across the street, watching Donavan climb out of the window. *Bad little nigga. Somebody sure 'nuff spared the rod on that one.* Mickey had driven back over to the house to put a couple nice clean bullets in the assistant DA's new family. Then Isaac pulled up.

He banged his fist against his forehead. "Stupid, stupid, stupid." How could he have forgotten that Isaac's son still lived in Dayton? Well, because Isaac didn't write and didn't call, that's how. "See," he wanted to shout at Isaac. "You didn't keep in touch like you promised, and your son was almost dead. You shouldn't have played me, Isaac."

Mickey chewed on his nubby nails. "So now what am I going to do?" He hated Charles Douglas III with all that was evil in him. He wanted to hurt him. Give him some pain to carry with him for the few years he had left on earth. The man had been dogging him for years. It was Charles who caused the FBI to investigate him. Charles who stood in court and told the judge that Mickey was a menace to society. Charles who tried to block his bail.

"He's no better than a dog," Charles had told the judge. Just like his dope fiend mother, had said. But Mickey had shown her. Sometimes, when he was feeling real low, he liked to remember the day his worthless mother had come to him begging for some crack.

Oh, she needed him now. She said she was sorry about the way she had treated him. Of course he wasn't a failure, wasn't a loser. "Thanks for the apology, Mom. Now get your dope fiend self on the street and work for your drugs like the rest of my hookers."

Mickey laughed out loud. He had to put his hand over his mouth so Isaac and Nina wouldn't hear him. The look on his mother's face that day was priceless. He'd pay money to see it again.

Charles had called him a dog. Well, he could call him a stalker now. Mickey liked the sound of that. Yeah, the night stalker. He just never imagined that the DA's woman would be Isaac's baby's mama. Talk about total turn about. This girl needed to pick which side of the law she was going to pull

her men from. She was probably a bad mother just like his
had been. Maybe she was the informant that got Isaac sent
up all those years ago. Maybe offing her would be doing
Isaac a favor. Paying him back for all the advice and upstart
money.

"Don't waste tears over that one, Isaac. I'll have a bullet in
her before you send off the next child support check,"
Mickey whispered with a smile on his face as he thought of
the good deed he was about to do for Isaac. But then the
smile faded as he realized that relieving Nina Lewis of her
life meant Isaac would have to watch the kid. Isaac had
been his mentor. He'd taught him everything he knew about
running the streets. Now he was on top. He commanded respect. No way was he going to give the man who helped him
get where he was today the full time responsibility of raising
Chucky.

Mickey drove away from the house wondering where
Charles's mother lived.

# 9

An hour had passed before Isaac realized that he'd forgotten Donavan. He slammed his fist on the steering wheel. Here he was disappointing his son again. "God, I make my own self sick."

Isaac knew the signs of a hoodlum. Shoot, he had given new meaning to the term. And his son was heading in that direction fast. He needed a firm hand. A good beating every now and then would keep him on the straight and unhandcuffed way. But Nina wanted to coddle the boy. Breastfeed him until he drowned on the eleven-year-old milk she was dishing up.

He wanted to turn around. Go back and get his son. But he didn't have the strength to see Nina again. Couldn't look at that engagement ring and remain calm. He barely got out of there without smashing his fist against the porch banister as it was. If he went back now, Nina would feel vindicated in all her rightness if he lost his cool and got to acting typical; with fist smashing into something.

Anyway, he was still fuming from her last comment. She had the audacity to tell him to *be a man and handle his business.* What had he been doing for the last five years? Forget all this drama. He didn't need Nina Lewis and he certainly didn't need Usually Wrong.

Isaac considered that maybe it was time for Donavan to move in with him. He'd approached the subject with Nina on several occasions, but she always resisted. Her son needed his mommy. And anyway, what would she do with all that breast milk if she let her son grow up and become a man? Man, ha. His son was a hoodrat. "Like father, like son. Is that the way it's going to be, Donny-boy?"

Isaac was no fool. He'd come from the streets. The streets of Dayton still sung his praises. He knew a potential state employee when he saw one. Donavan might as well have the license plate making tools in his hands right now.

But Isaac hadn't said 'Yes' to Jesus just so he could stand in a courtroom and watch the gavel come down on his only son. He'd deal with the situation. Put Donavan back on an eleven-year-old good-kid kind of path. But not this weekend. He was drained. He would go home, lick his wounds and prepare his Sunday morning sermon.

The cushion of his bed did little to calm his troubled mind. He was tired, but didn't want to sleep. *They* were on his bed again. Pressing on him, weighing down his mattress. *Scream,* he told himself. But one of them had clamped his mouth shut. Prickly tentacles massaged his scalp, taking him under. Dragging him into the abyss. One awful night in Isaac's jail cell, God had allowed him to experience hell. Actually, he had a reunion down there. Met up with all the people he had sent to eternity, in one way or another. Now, these demons thought they had free reign. Thought they could just bring him back whenever they were having a slow night. *Oh, Lord, help me. I'm having another nightmare!*

"Look at you. Big, bad, Isaac Walker crying for help."

*Oh, God; not again! Not this again!* But as he lifted his

head, he knew the demons had won. Isaac was spending another nightmarish night in hell. Sweat drizzled from Isaac's coal black hair. It clung to his nose like icicles. Could he live through another night of God-awful torment? Evil evaded his space and demanded his attention.

Destroyer, that old enemy demon taunted him. "What's wrong, Ike-man? You're not allowed to talk to us no more? Don't you want to come out and play?"

Isaac didn't open his mouth. The torment was worse when he talked back. He tried not to take in the suffocating smell of death and decay. No use. The odor slithered up his nostrils and crawled down his throat, gagging him. He tried not to think about his brother, Donavan, or his ex-girlfriend, Valerie, being tormented in this place for eternity. But that was useless too. Tears creased the corners of his eyes. It was all his fault. If he had been a better brother; if he had left Valerie alone, maybe she would have gone back to church and rededicated her life to the Lord. Life was full of coulda-shoulda-wouldas. He'd go back if he could, right the wrongs. "Oh God, if only I could change it!"

Destroyer's heat stained breath beat down on him as he lay on the scorching, hot floor of hell. "Serve your daddy again, Isaac. Let Lucifer help you change it."

"Never!" Isaac said as he stood up.

Two of Satan's henchmen brought Donavan's mangled form into what the demons called the Fun Room. Although the demons had plenty of fun, none of the inhabitants of this room had any. They were too busy having their limbs torn off and being used for target practice to have any fun.

Isaac fell on his knees. "Help me, Lord. I don't know what you want." A sob caught in his throat. Tears mingled with sweat. "Don't know how to fix it."

Destroyer's flesh devouring fangs cut into Isaac's back as he pulled him off his knees. "Shut up, fool. Ain't no God down here. You pray in hell, you pray to Lucifer."

Isaac's back ached as Destroyer dug into him, but his mind was made up. He would serve the Lord with his last breath. No devil in hell would stop his praise.

"The Lord is everywhere, beholding both good and evil," Isaac shouted.

Destroyer pimp-smacked Isaac and flung him against the wall of lost souls. The wall was sticky from the heat. The souls that had been encased inside the wall seemed to scream out to him; begging him to save them. But the wall was so sticky, Isaac didn't even know how he would get himself unglued from it, let alone open up the wall and begin pulling lost souls out of its God forsaken clutches.

Isaac tried to pull himself off of the wall of lost souls, but he couldn't get free. The cries inside the wall tormented him. Isaac felt defeated. He just wanted to give up and remain attached to this wall.

Then Destroyer began taunting him again. "Watch this, Isaac. Then you tell me again how your God is everywhere."

Isaac was still struggling, trying to get away from the wall when he looked at Destroyer. Destroyer pointed in the direction of the two demons that were tormenting his brother. But it was no longer Donavan, his brother, standing between two demons with arms stretched wide, but Donavan, his son. *When would this nightmare end?*

Destroyer lifted his sword and Donavan looked at Isaac and cried, "Help me, Daddy. Help me."

Desperation hit Isaac like a hurricane. Knocked him over, left him for dead. "Oh, God, don't let this happen. This is my son, Lord."

Destroyer's blade dug into Donavan's chest.

"Aaaaaarrgh!"

Destroyer laughed then cut into Donavan again.

With a resolve to get his son away from these monsters, Isaac knuckled up and mean-mugged his opponent. Nostrils flaring, mac-daddy stance in place, he told them, "Leave him alone. I'm the one you want."

Destroyer snapped his crust-laden fingers. Two grizzly looking demons pulled Isaac off the wall and threw him around like they were Hulk Hogan in his pre-arthritic days.

*Oh, it's on. Let one of 'em drop me. I'm gon' beat him like he stole something.* But before Isaac could get his rumble on, a bell went off. His first thought was to find the judges and ask them to stop ringing that bell. Ain't no sense letting the bad guys win when he wasn't tired yet. He quickly realized that the bell was ringing inside his head. Probably from that punch he had just taken.

When the demons got tired of slapping him around, they slung him on the floor next to Donavan. Now, both he and his son screamed in agony as the hell-bent demons ripped through their bodies.

"Aaaaaarrgh! Aaaaaarrgh!" Isaac screamed while jumping around in his bed. The sudden movement jarred him. Isaac awoke panting. He gasped for air and reached for the telephone and dialed.

The phone rang three times before a groggy voice said, "Hello."

"Put Donavan on the phone," he told Nina. No time for acting like he had manners. He needed to make sure his son was still alive.

Nina looked at the clock on her nightstand. Three a.m. "Isaac do you know what time it is?"

"Nina, please. Just go get Donavan for me. I won't call your house this early in the morning again. But right now, I need to speak to my son."

Putting the phone down, she pulled back the covers and got out of her warm bed. Yawning as she headed to her son's room, Nina called out, "Donavan. Donavan."

Donavan was closing the window he'd just climbed back

into when he heard his mother calling. Quickly discarding his jeans and faking a yawn he said, "Yeah."

Outside his door, Nina told him, "Come get the phone. Your daddy wants to talk to you."

"Aw, Mom, I'm sleep. Can't it wait 'til morning?"

"No, Donavan. It sounds important."

Donavan snatched the door open and stormed down the hall to his mother's room. He picked up the phone and growled into the receiver, "Yeah, what is it?"

"What have you been doing?" Isaac demanded.

Donavan let out a bored yawn. "What do people do at three in the morning, Dad?"

"Don't you get smart with me. I'll come back down there and give you the beaten you should have gotten last night."

"But I didn't get it; did I, Dad? And why not? Because you left me. Didn't think one more thing about me after you got mad at Mom, did you?"

Isaac sighed. "I'm sorry about that, Donavan. But I need to know, son. What did you do after I left last night?"

Rolling his eyes, Donavan told Isaac, "I went to bed. What else could I do?"

"Donavan, don't lie to me. This is important." Isaac knew with everything in him that something bad was going on with his son, and the thought terrified him.

Donavan's voice boomed back with anger. "Look, don't call here accusing me. You don't know what I've been doing, and you don't care. So get off my back!"

When the dial tone sounded in Isaac's ear, all he could do was shake his head. Chip off the ol' block indeed.

# 10

Donavan didn't find JC until Saturday afternoon. He was in a "conference" with bad luck Baby Dee and Mark Smith. Baby Dee was a high school drop out who'd once convinced his best friend to rob a pawnshop on Third Street. The owner was a mean something who didn't believe in giving up his money without a fight. He locked the door and commenced to beating Baby Dee and his friend with a baseball bat. They pulled the plug on his friend a week later at Good Samaritan.

It had always been a mystery to Donavan why a smart college student like Mark Smith still hung around JC. Sure, they had been best friends throughout high school, but Mark was in his third year of college. JC was on his third felony. Absolutely no future in that friendship.

"Man, my scholarship is busted. If I don't get some money quick, I can forget about graduating next year."

So that was it. Mark needs money, so he came to the thug-and-loan for help. Good luck cashing that check.

JC looked toward Donavan. "Hey, Shortie. Can I catch up with you later? Me and my boys got business to discuss."

"I'm staying." Donavan wouldn't be put off. "Mark needs money, and so do I. If you've got a solution other than pulling the lent out of your pockets, I want to hear it."

JC laughed. "All right, Shortie. I'll cut you in."

A young girl and her baby were hugged close together on the dirty brown carpet of a crack house on Fifth Street. She had a pipe in her left hand. The baby lay crying, cradled in the crevice of her other arm. The pipe was receiving more attention than the baby.

An old gray-headed man slumped against the wall next to her. The dirty pipe he held looked more like an extended member of his dirty hand.

Donavan stood in front of ten pounds of gold chains with a VCR in his hands. He looked around the room. It was empty except for a chipped and stained wooden table with three padded chairs and a pullout drawer underneath the table top. "I want to trade this VCR," Donavan said after taking in his surroundings.

"I can't touch it, young blood. I got too many VCRs as it is," Mr. T, the gold chain wearing drug dealer said.

This was Baby Dee's bright idea. *"Let's rob the crack house down the street and split the money."* The baseball bat beating probably shook loose the last good brain cells the boy had, and here he was following the counsel of a brain dead dummy. *"You go in and distract him, Donavan. We'll bum rush him before he knows what's up."*

"But it's all I've got. Come on man . . . I need this," Donavan begged.

"Cash money, man. You think my supplier's gon' take a VCR when he comes collecting his money?"

Donavan stood there for a moment longer. Sweat ran down his forehead as he gave his best imitation of a body twitch. The boy was good. Looked like a regular crack head. His eyes pleaded with Mr. T. "I need it, man."

"Alright, alright." He eyed his customer's arm. "Gimme that gold watch, and you can get your high on."

Not just any watch, but a sixth grade graduation present from his dad. Donavan looked at the gold band. His dad had even had it inscribed 'God is great in you,' but the watch was a lie. His father was a liar too. He needed the money JC promised. He was thinking about running away and everyone knows that a runaway needed money to set out on his own. If he had to steal to get it, who could blame him? He was just following in his old man's footsteps. Donavan unlatched the watch and slowly handed it over to the dope man, Mr. T. "I'm gonna buy this back from you. Okay?"

Mr. T read the inscription and laughed out loud as he handed his customer his medicine. As Donavan reached out for his ounce of pleasure, JC and Baby Dee rushed Mr. T.

They shoved the dope man against the wall. Baby Dee stood in front of Mr. T with his gun trained on his chest. JC positioned himself next to the victim, his gun at the man's temple.

"Give it up, homeboy. This is payday," JC told him.

Mr. T put his hands up and tried to move his head away from the gun. "Are you stupid? You know this is Mickey's money."

"Mickey don't scare me," Baby Dee told him. "He's getting ready to be some dude named Bubba's date to the prom."

"Don't count Mickey out so soon," Mr. T warned them.

"Shut up." JC hit him with the butt of the gun. "Let go of the money or say your prayers."

Mr. T pointed at the wooden table and told them, "The money is in the drawer underneath the table top. Take it; it's your funeral."

Donavan grabbed his watch and ran out of the house. He jumped in the white Chevy in front of the crack house. Mark was behind the wheel. The boy was shaking worse than David Chappelle in *Blue Streak*. This was definitely not his thing. Donavan wanted to tell him to jump out of the car and run home. Go back to college. Get out while the getting was good. But if Mark left, he'd be stuck there with JC and under-educated Baby Dee. No, he needed to make sure he got out of that place alive. His mother was making mac & cheese for dinner tonight. Mmm, good.

# 11

Seeing his brother in hell again caused Isaac to want to slash out. It didn't help matters when his brother's face had turned into his own son's.

Oh, and every time he thought of Nina's last comment, *"Be a man, Isaac,"* he just wanted to break something. Guess that's why she's marrying Charles. He must be a man; able to handle all his issues.

"Well, maybe he never had a father who killed his mother. Did you ever think of that, Ms. Nina Lewis? No, no. You didn't think about that. Too busy judging me." Isaac was having this conversation with himself as he pulled up at the church job site. He got out of his car and searched for MacMillian.

MacMillian saw Isaac first and did a fast walk toward the trailer. "I don't want any trouble," he said as Isaac approached.

Isaac raised his hand. "I come in peace. I'm looking for somebody. I thought you might be able to help me."

MacMillian stood in silence with his hand on the trailer door.

"That guy, Marvin. Can you give me his address?"

"What do you want with him? You've already cost him his job; isn't that enough for you?"

"Look, I'll be honest with you. The man is my father. We've kind of been on bad terms lately. But I want to talk with him." Isaac smiled. "Help me out. Okay?"

MacMillian hesitated for a minute, then snapped his fingers. "That's right. Marvin's last name is Walker. When I met you, I thought you looked familiar."

"I look nothing like him," Isaac said roughly, then with a slight smile he added, "I take after my mother's side of the family."

MacMillian gave up the address and Isaac was back on the Dan Ryan Freeway. Fifteen minutes later, Isaac was in front of Usually Wrong's house. He couldn't have wished the poverty of the Westside on a more deserving person. Isaac could see a drug deal going down in the breezeway. He wished that someone would sell Usually Wrong something that would send his heart racing, pumping out of control until he keeled over dead. A little dramatic, but that's what his dreams were made of.

Isaac had been saved and serving the Lord for seven years now, but he still hadn't learned to forgive. He'd met many bitter, unforgiving, so-called Christians and swore that he would not be like them. But he still hadn't been able to let go of the past. He was in need of prayer for this issue and hoped that someone was praying for him.

Walking toward Marvin's broken down front door, Isaac heard something that made him change direction.

"Cynda, girl I ain't playing with you. You better give me my money."

It had to be her. Not many people named their children Cynda, rather than plain ol' Cindy. He only knew one woman with that name. The woman he had wronged. He took off running toward the breezeway where the voices were coming from.

When he reached his destination, Cynda was clutching her poison, screaming at the big bellied man who'd given it to her. "I already paid you."

"Trick, please. What you put out wasn't worth half the yank I gave you."

Standing there, watching Cynda clutch a baggy full of crack, sent Isaac's mind reeling back in time. Years ago, he had watched her snort cocaine with an old friend. That same so-called friend was now Cynda's pimp. He remembered telling Spoony to give him fifty cents, and he could have Cynda. Isaac hung his head. His memories weren't sweet. They were the kind of thing that young children woke up screaming and running to their mommy's room to get away from. But how could he get away from himself? From yesterday?

Years of smoking dope and turning tricks had taken a bit of a toll on Cynda. She was still beautiful. But she now had a few splotches on her face. He'd never seen a woman as flawless as the one before him had once been. It took crack to put a pimple on her cheeks.

Defiantly, Cynda told her pusher, "You got what you wanted. Now, get out of my way before I stick this in your throat." She brandished a rusty box cutter and her enemy backed off.

"You're crazy, you know that? Don't come around here no more." He backed into Isaac as he left the breezeway.

"Cynda," Isaac almost whispered her name. He was ashamed of the manner in which he'd found her.

She turned, glazed eyes in Isaac's direction. Silence held them for a brief span of time. "What do you want?" she asked while shoving the baggy in the pocket of her mini, mini skirt.

Isaac walked toward her. "Cynda, you don't want to live like this. I'd like to help you."

Laughing in his face, Cynda closed her knife and put it in her jeans jacket.

Her laughter wasn't the ha-ha funny kind. It was mean and sinister. Isaac couldn't blame her. He even understood the hatred he saw in her dark eyes.

"Do you need anything? What can I do for you?" Isaac asked.

Her hands were on her hips as she posed seductively for him. "That's usually my line."

"Look, Cynda. I was horrible to you. I know that. I just want to help you out of the mess you've gotten yourself into."

She harrumphed. "Oh, I had help getting myself into *this mess*."

He opened his mouth, then closed it. What could he say? He had sold her to the devil.

As if she knew where his thoughts had gone, she told him, "I've come up in the world, Isaac. I get up to a thousand a night for my services."

He wanted to ask why she was in the breezeway giving her stuff way if she was so high priced. But he knew—that monkey on her back.

She strutted over to him and smiled wickedly. "A far cry from fifty cents wouldn't you say?"

He hung his head, then lifted it and stared into Cynda's hateful eyes. He hoped the remorse he felt showed on his face. "I'm sorry about that."

She tilted her head back and hocked up some spit.

Isaac wiped his face with his shirtsleeve as Cynda took off running out of the breezeway and down the street.

He wanted to run after her. Help her to see that he truly wanted to help. Somebody needed to knock some sense in her head. Okay, one of those knocks would be for the spit she flung in his face, but the rest would be for her own good.

He turned and looked at his father's house and reminded himself that he had bigger fish to fry. He needed to deal with his own issues.

Strutting back to the dilapidated house with determination and a twinge of unchecked anger, Isaac told himself that Nina was wrong about him. He could deal with his issues.

Stepping on the porch, Isaac prepared himself to bang on the door. Just then, two little girls with matching pink and blue ribbons, and cotton jogging suits came rushing out of the door and ran past him. Must be twins; they looked too much alike. They looked like Donavan. He turned back to the door and greeted the big-bellied form of Usually Wrong. He had on dirty blue jeans and a wife-beater, go figure. Pushing his hands in his pockets, Isaac gave him a head nod.

Usually Wrong stepped onto the porch and yelled, "Derricka and Kivonna, don't you run off nowhere."

Noticing the wedding band on his left hand, Isaac asked, "Who are they?"

Marvin smiled with his lips, but it didn't quite meet his eyes. "My daughters."

"Look at you, *daddio*." Marvin didn't respond, thereby angering Isaac all the more. "What you doing? Over here molesting them sweet little girls?"

That got his attention. "I never molested you or your brother."

"No. You were always interested in the ladies. Which brings me to the reason I'm here." Anger penetrated every pore of Isaac's body. He shook from it. "I just wanted to come over here and thank you for the legacy of woman beating and womanizing that you gave me. But I also want you to know that with the help of Jesus, I'm conquering all that mess. I will never be the man you are." He pulled his hands out of his pockets and walked off the porch.

Marvin reached out and touched Isaac's shoulder to turn him around. "Wait a minute, son."

Isaac snatched away from him and snarled. "Don't you ever call me son."

Marvin's eyes were filled with unshed tears. "I'm sorry, Isaac. Can you forgive me?"

"*Sorry*? I tell you what. I'll forgive you when my mother and brother forgive you."

"I don't know what else to say, Isaac." The tears were flowing down his face now as he continued, "I have lived with what I did for so long. I just want peace now."

Isaac almost hit him. "At least you're living. You arrogant, no-good—"

The girls ran back to the porch. "Who's this, Daddy?" the taller girl asked.

Marvin wiped the tears from his face, looked at Isaac and then back at his children. "An old friend."

"Well, he looks a lot like the picture of your son on our mantle," Kivonna told him.

"Yeah, he does," Marvin answered. "Go on in the house, girls."

Isaac walked toward his car. Marvin lingered on the porch watching him. When he opened the car door, he turned back to Marvin. "I'll tell you what. You're not going to be able to get my mother's forgiveness. She's in heaven and you'll never see her again. But when you get to hell, and actually see how Donavan is tortured and tormented, I want you to tell him how sorry you are. And see if it makes a difference."

Isaac stood in front of the congregation. They were using a school building for Sunday services while the new facility was being built. He hadn't been able to get his mind off his son all weekend. As sure as he knew his name was Isaac Walker, he knew that his son was headed for trouble; just as he had been at that same age.

He hadn't been able to shake off the rage he'd felt after seeing his useless father either. When Isaac reached back into his history, all of his trials, all of his tribulations started with that man. He'd prayed all Saturday about his son and the situation with Usually Wrong. As a matter of fact, one could say that his son and father had inspired his message for today.

He looked out at the five hundred plus people that gathered to praise God in this gymnasium/Sunday sanctuary. The congregation sat in the bleachers, while the pulpit stood below the basketball hoop. The people that attended these services weren't interested in showing off expensive suits or brand new dresses. They came to this church to forget about the lifetime of bad decisions that consumed their lives. But maybe they shouldn't forget. Maybe they should spend time thinking about their problems so that their children won't have to live through them. "I want to talk to you today about generational curses."

That's the way it went. Isaac preached based on his sorrows, and the congregation responded. He finished his sermon, shook hands with the members of the congregation as they left the school building and then walked toward the locker room. Isaac sat down on one of the benches and truly thought about this latter glory that God promised. He hoped it was like the latter rain that swept in like a flood and washed away the residue his former life had left behind. Isaac took the picture of Nina and Donavan out of his wallet and stared at it.

A knock on the door pulled Isaac away from his thoughts. He put the picture on the bench next to him and said, "Come in."

The door creaked as it slowly opened to allow one of the prettiest chocolate delights this side of the Mississippi to enter. Isaac stood to greet her. He needed something good to happen to him today. He didn't know what she wanted, but he was ready to say yes to almost anything.

She had long black hair, which Isaac liked. The kind of hair a man could run his hands through. He was convinced that Nina kept her hair short just to get on his last nerve.

"I'm Cassandra Davis." She walked closer to Isaac with an outstretched hand. "Bishop Sumler asked me to see you after service."

Isaac snapped his finger, as if just remembering something important. "You're our new praise leader, right?"

She smiled. They shook hands. "I'm still trying to decide which church I will be joining, but I enjoyed your sermon today. You're very motivational."

"Thank you. Have a seat, Ms. Davis," he said as if they were in an office, rather than a locker room. When she was seated on the same bench as he, Isaac said, "So, tell me a little bit about your background. Like, where did you live before moving to Chicago, and why'd you decide to move?"

"Well, I used to live in Louisville, Kentucky. I had been attending Christian United Tabernacle, but I needed a change."

"Sometimes change is good."

She pointed at the picture that lay next to Isaac. "Is that your wife and son?"

Isaac turned, picked up the picture and stared at it for a moment. Actually, a long moment. While he stared, he thought about the man that would soon have his family. He wondered if Charles Douglas III knew how blessed he was. "This is my son," he told her as he put the picture back down. "But I'm not married."

She folded her hands in her lap, but remained silent.

Looking at this woman across from him, Isaac wondered if she could be the one for him. Maybe Nina was not meant to be with him forever. Maybe she wasn't part of the equation with him and God. If nothing else had convinced him, that engagement ring sure should have. "Are you hungry? Would you like to grab something to eat?"

Coyly, Cassandra said, "Oh, are you going to take me to lunch? Pastor Marks told me his wife would kill him, if he took me to lunch without her."

"Well, see, that's the difference between me and Pastor Marks." Isaac smiled as he finished his statement. "I'm not married and very free for lunch."

# 12

"How many pancakes do you want?" Nina asked. Donavan rolled over in bed and told his mother, "I'm not hungry."

Nina's mouth hung slack. She walked to Donavan's bed and sat down. "Since when do you turn down my pancakes? I've got plenty of cinnamon in them."

"I'm not feeling well. I don't think I'm going to school today." He held his stomach as if a shooting pain had just gone through it.

Nina touched her son's forehead, "You don't have a fever. Your eyes are bright and clear." She touched his stomach; it didn't feel bloated or tight. She pulled the cover off of him. "Boy, get your butt out of this bed and get up for school."

He snatched the cover back over himself. "No!"

Stunned once again by her son's behavior, Nina sat in silence, wondering if Isaac had been right. Did her son need his father more than his mother? Was a firm hand better than open arms? "Donavan, what's going on with you? Lately, you seem so distant."

He didn't respond. Just sucked in his breath.

"In church yesterday, you were walking the halls while Pastor McKinley preached. You never used to do things like that." She bent down and touched his arm. "I'm worried about you. Talk to me; okay?"

He threw the covers back and blew out a big gust of evil pre-teenage wind. "I just didn't feel like being at church. Why do you have to make a federal case out of everything?" He stood and tried to walk out of his room.

Nina grabbed his arm. "Look, I don't know what's wrong with you, but let's get one thing straight. This is my house, and you will respect me in here. You got me?"

Pulling his arm away, he told her, "Yeah, I got you. Are you still going to fix breakfast?"

Calming herself, Nina said, "Yes. Go take a shower and I'll meet you in the kitchen in a minute."

Before she went to the kitchen, Nina knelt at the living room couch and prayed. "Father, things aren't going well for me and Donavan. I really need your help. Oh, Jesus, I sure could use a little wisdom right now." She got up and fixed her son his cinnamon pancakes and tried desperately to pull him out of his shell.

After failing to get inside her reluctant pre-teen's head, Nina sat at her computer and tried to get into Ramona's. The heroine in Nina's third book was still struggling with God's ability to forgive people who had abortions. She was stuck. Called it writer's block, but in truth, it was a faith block. Admitting that to herself stung.

The phone rang. Nina normally didn't answer it when she was writing, but she had no answers for Ramona. Nina wanted to scream at the fictional character. Tell her that she shouldn't have done it. Her life was all messed up because of that one single incident. *Now, go out and live life to the fullest with the knowledge of that, Ramona girl.*

She picked up the phone on the third ring. "Hello, this is

Nina," she told the caller as if some other woman would be answering her phone at ten o'clock on a Monday morning.

"Hey, girl; what's up?"

It was Elizabeth, and Nina was about ready to explode all over her. "About time I'm hearing from you. My goodness. I've only called you about ten times."

"Calm down. I was on the last leg of my tour when I got your message. I was too tired to pick up the phone. Sorry. I'm here now."

Nina smiled. The tabloids called Elizabeth Underwood a gospel singing sensation, but she simply called her *friend*. Best friend. They'd met at The Rock Christian Fellowship. Nina still attended The Rock, but Elizabeth had moved away from Dayton several years earlier. Her husband, Kenneth, had been in the World Trade Center during the terrorists' attack in 2001. Elizabeth had thought that Kenneth was lost to her forever, and she had crumbled. But Elizabeth was strong; she was a fighter. And God had restored her and brought her husband back home.

"Well, I've got some news," Nina stated.

"Don't get me all knotted up on the inside. Spill it," Elizabeth told her.

Nina played with her engagement ring. "I don't know if I want to tell you now. You kept me waiting, so I think I might call you back tomorrow to let you know that I just got engaged."

Elizabeth screamed. "Oh, my God. How did he ask you?"

"He actually asked me a while ago. I just hadn't said anything because I didn't want to upset Donavan."

"Why would Donavan be upset?" Elizabeth sounded confused. "He's always wanted you and Isaac to get back together. I would think he would be ecstatic."

Nina shook her head as if Elizabeth could see her from across the telephone line. "Not you too. Elizabeth, I've been dating Charles for several months now. You know that."

"Oh," she said flatly. "I didn't think it was serious."

Nina put her hands on her hips. "But you thought I had something serious going on with Isaac?"

"No, nothing like that. I just know that Isaac has been planning to marry you since the day he left prison. I just thought you finally gave in."

"That will never happen," Nina assured her friend.

"Alright, excuse me for being wrong. But tell me, Nina, when did you suddenly fall in love with Charles Douglas?"

Nina slouched in her seat and grinned goofy-like as she thought about Charles. "I don't know. I think I'm attracted to how responsible he is. He's loyal and he's a nice man, Elizabeth. Truth be told, I think he will be good for Donavan also. You know, give him some stability."

They talked a little longer about wedding plans, Elizabeth's family, and Nina's love-hate relationship with Isaac Walker. When they finally hung up, Nina turned off her computer and went for a walk.

Donavan watched as his mother walked down Oxford. He sat perched on an abandoned car. The school bus had left an hour ago. She didn't even notice that he didn't get on it. Why didn't she just leave him alone? Just run off with her boyfriend? She didn't care about him. Didn't even want to know how his insides were eaten up with guilt over following behind JC and his crew.

He still couldn't believe that he risked his life for three hundred bucks. That was the amount JC gave him. How much his services had been worth. He might only be eleven—almost twelve, but he knew that three hundred bucks wasn't going to get him far.

"Hey, kid. Get off of my car." A fat man with a gun was standing on his porch hollering at Donavan.

Donavan jumped down from the hood of the car and ran. He had no plans the rest of his day; had no idea what he would do until he could go back home. So, he just wandered the streets, trying to get as far away from the route his mother had taken as possible. A few blocks over, he ran into a couple of teenagers standing behind an abandoned house, smoking cigarettes and shooting dice. Donavan didn't want to shoot dice. His father had told him too many times that his uncle had been murdered over a dice game. So, dice were out of the question for him.

"What up?" Donavan asked with a wave of his hand as he sat down on the back porch and watched them. He figured if he could strike up a conversation, they might let him hang with them for the rest of the day. But the three guys were already talking about something. Donavan heard the name Mickey Jones and his mouth went dry.

"Man, did you hear that Mickey got took for five thou the other night," the tall, scraggly one asked.

The guy with the cigarette took it out of his mouth, blew out smoke and said, "I wish it had been me. I could use five thou right about now. My mom's house is about to be foreclosed on."

"Naw, man, you don't want that money." The third and final guy speaking was shorter than the other two, but he was muscular; built like a fighter. The fighter continued, "Heard Mickey is looking for those so and sos. He's going to kill them with his bare hands."

Donavan had nothing to contribute to this conversation. He stepped off the back porch and left. As he walked around the neighborhood, Donavan realized that he was a chump. Three hundred dollars wasn't worth this kind of stress. He couldn't even run away with that little bit of money. He might as well go buy himself a Sean John outfit and wait to die.

After all, according to those guys in the back of that house, Mickey Jones was looking for the so and sos that robbed him.

# 13

Cassandra had decided to join his church rather than Pastor Marks's. Isaac was happy about that. He found himself smiling when he saw her again, which of course, was at Wednesday night Bible Study. Actually, he saw her on Tuesday also. He told Cassandra that he and Keith were going to be working late. She showed up at his office with smothered pork chops, cabbage, mac & cheese and some peach cobbler. A brother got fed good.

Now she was walking over to him with some of that left over peach cobbler. Service had been good. Bishop preached well, but none of that compared to Cassandra's peach cobbler.

Keith had told Isaac that he needed to watch out. He thought Cassandra was being too good, too fast. Well, Nina wasn't trying to be good to him. Nina was jumping the broom with some other dude. Cassandra could be as good to him as she wanted.

"Just let me know if you have to work late again. There's no sense in you having to worry about dinner. I'll bring something to you," Cassandra told Isaac with a smile on her face and a look in her eyes that told Isaac all he needed to know about how she was feeling about him.

Isaac sat in the kitchen in the back of the church wolfing down peach cobbler and thinking how sweet it was to be treated like a king again. He gave Cassandra a smile that showed off his dimples. "As good as you cook, you can hook a brother up, even when I'm not working late."

Cassandra stood next to Isaac, silent, but pleased.

Bishop Sumler picked that moment to rush into the kitchen. "Isaac, get your bags packed," he said without acknowledging Cassandra.

"What's up, Bishop?" Isaac swallowed his last bite of cobbler.

"We need to get over to my church in West Virginia. The members are calling me right and left. They say they'll all leave, if I don't fire their pastor."

"Pastor Marks?" Cassandra asked with a puzzled look on her face. "Why would the congregation want to get rid of him?"

Isaac knew Pastor Marks, and had a pretty good idea why the congregation wanted him fired. But he wasn't going to tell Cassandra all that he knew. Pastor Marks's reputation was another reason Isaac was glad that Cassandra decided to join his church rather than Marks's.

Bishop put his arm around Cassandra and looked at Isaac with a smile on his face. "So, I hear that my goddaughter has been feeding you real good."

Isaac stammered. "T-this is your goddaughter? You didn't tell us that."

Patting Cassandra on the shoulder, Bishop said, "Cassandra doesn't like to make a big deal of the fact that she's my goddaughter. But, take my word for it, she is something special," Bishop said to Isaac then turned to Cassandra. "Can you give us a few minutes to talk?"

Like an obedient child, Cassandra said, "Sure, Bishop. I'll sit at the table over there," she pointed to the left of them where a group of women sat, "and get to know some of the women at your church."

When Cassandra was gone, Bishop turned back to Isaac. "This thing with Pastor Marks needs to be solved."

Some of these preachers reminded Isaac of street hustlers. Isaac knew exactly how to deal with hustlers and he also knew that that was the reason Bishop wanted him to go to West Virginia with him. Isaac truly did want to go with Bishop, but regrettably, he had other obligations. He needed to pick up Donavan this weekend. He needed to talk to his son before he got caught up. "I can't go. Not this time. I've got to pick my son up this weekend."

Bishop raised his hands. "Now, son, I know you've got family obligations, but this is important."

And Donavan wasn't?

"I need you on this trip, Isaac. Pastor Marks is not always a reasonable man."

Understatement though that was, Isaac still had responsibilities, and he wasn't about to leave them to good ol' Charlie. "Bishop, you know I'd love to help you, but my house is a mess. I've been working double-time all week long. And I have got to see Donavan this weekend."

Bishop Sumler called Cassandra back over. When she stood in front of them he said, "Isaac needs his house straightened up. You wouldn't mind helping him out, now would you, Sister Davis?"

Cassandra opened her mouth, but Bishop rushed on. "It's for the good of the ministry. Isaac, run home and pack your bags. Give, Sister Davis your keys. She'll make sure you come home to a clean house."

Isaac looked toward Cassandra.

She smiled. "I don't mind. Go take care of your business."

"Bishop, there's still my son to consider."

Bishop waved a dismissive hand in the air. "We'll pick him up on our way back. Help me handle this mess, Isaac. You'll still be able to get Donavan on Saturday."

He wasn't going to win this one. Might as well go home and pack.

# 14

The nine-hour drive to West Virginia wore out Isaac. Needless to say, by Thursday morning, he was cranky. By the time Pastor Ronald Marks strutted his well-paid self into his elegant mahogany laden office, Isaac was in a state of anger.

In his late thirties, Ron was graying prematurely. Probably from all that late night partying he did when his wife and children went to bed. He leaned against his sturdy desk, crossed his legs and smiled at Isaac and Bishop. "So, what brings you boys all the way down here?"

Bishop smiled back at him, crossed his legs, then told him, "You know why we're here, Ronald. Looks like you've exposed yourself to the wrong woman."

Ronald dismissed the thought with a wave of his hand. "I've got it under control. One more week, and everything will be back to normal at Faith Temple."

Under the leadership of Pastor Marks, Faith Temple had grown from a shabby two hundred member church to more than two thousand. His members didn't earn a lot, but they trusted that God would make a way, so they paid their tithes and offerings faithfully. The church grossed about fifteen million dollars annually, one of the largest in Bishop Sumler's fellowship; thus, the arrogance they were receiving from Pastor Marks right now. Who would touch the golden child?

Isaac shook his head. Ain't no hustle like a Holy Ghost hustle.

"What makes you so sure that you can fix this situation?" Bishop asked hopefully.

"I told the little tramp to get rid of it."

*It* was the baby Pastor Marks had planted in sixteen-year-old Tiffany Miliner's stomach. AKA, the little tramp.

Rage. Isaac knew it well. He just didn't know how to calm it once it was upon him. Red. He wanted to kill this animal. He rubbed his head with his palm while silently telling himself to calm down.

"What's wrong, Brother Walker?" Marks taunted.

Isaac ignored him and prayed for patience. Isaac wasn't fully delivered and this man was trying to get him in the flesh.

"Why you judging me, *brother*? I know you haven't forgotten about your little slip up with Denise Wilkerson so soon. She could have gotten pregnant, you know," Marks continued his taunt against Isaac.

"One mistake is not fifty. And if she'd have gotten pregnant, I would have taken care of my responsibility," Isaac told him as rage danced in his eyes.

Marks gave Isaac a 'yeah-right' glance. "You barely take care of the one you've got now." Walking over to the window, Marks turned his back on Isaac. First mistake. "Go get me a cup of coffee, and leave the grown folks' business to me and Bishop." Second mistake.

The beast in Isaac roared as he stood up and told Marks, "You don't know anything about my son. And instead of taunting me, I would think you'd be worried about what your behavior is doing to your family."

"I'm tired of your mouth," Marks said as he turned away from the window and swung at Isaac. Third mistake.

A gulping wind—whoosh, was knocked out of Marks as he hit the ground face first. His nose splattered blood all over the thick Persian rug. Isaac's fists hadn't seen warfare in quite some time. What's that thing about riding a bike? Well, it's the same for fighting, evidently. By the time Bishop Sumler pulled Isaac off Marks, Marks had received a good beat down and some wall-to-wall consultation. Not a dry cleaner in the world would be able to get all that blood out of Marks's linen suit.

"Th-this is outrageous!" Marks sputtered as he tried to get on his feet. The floor couldn't hold him steady, so he collapsed onto his knees. "I want his license revoked! What kind of preacher beats up on people?"

*What kind of preacher sleeps with half his congregation?* Isaac wanted to ask him, but he was busy trying to catch his breath. Whew, he was getting too old for this stuff.

"I bring in more money than any other preacher in this fellowship." Marks stood and pointed at Isaac. "So, if he isn't out of here, Faith Temple will find another Bishop to fellowship under by tomorrow."

"That's what I've been trying to tell you, Marks." Bishop walked over to Marks and adjusted his shirt and tie. "Like I said, it appears that you've exposed yourself to the wrong girl. Her parents are filing charges against you for statutory rape. You'll probably be in jail by tomorrow."

Another whoosh of air escaped Marks. He fell backward, all the while, trying to regain his balance. "Y-you can't let this happen, Bishop. That's why I joined your fellowship. You were supposed to protect me."

Bishop looked exhausted as he told him, "I can't protect you from yourself."

Isaac was tired of this whole scene. "Look, Marks, just clear your stuff out of this office and go home to your family. See if you can explain yourself to them before the police show up."

When Marks slithered out of the office, Isaac moved over to the window. Instead of taking in the hustle and bustle of the traffic below, Isaac stared at his hands. His eyes had a far away look. Remembering promises made, but not kept. "Oh, Lord, please forgive me."

He wasn't sorry for beating the living daylights out of Marks. He had to admit to himself and God that he'd do it again. But something deep within him was cracking. He wanted to beat MacMillan to death at that construction site, and had been a little disappointed when the man decided to resend that thieving bill. *Am I losing it, Father? Am I turning into the man I once was?*

"I guess you know you'll be giving the sermon at Faith Temple this Sunday," Bishop Sumler informed Isaac.

"What do you want me to do? Tell them how I beat their pastor half to death?"

Bishop walked over to Isaac and put his hand on his shoulder. "You can't let it get to you. The man is slime. Anybody would have done what you did."

Isaac wasn't sure about that. He shook his head and rubbed his chin. "I thought I was entering into something that would help the advancement of the Kingdom of God. But it seems like I left one game for another."

"Some days it seems like that, but you just have to hope that there's more good than bad in this thing." Sumler squeezed Isaac's shoulder. "Besides, this may be a door that God is opening for you."

Isaac turned to face his mentor. "What are you talking about?"

"You just work on your sermon. Let me worry about the rest." He turned and started walking out the door. Just before he left the room, Isaac heard him say, "Yep, this thing may just turn out for our good."

# 15

Charles's mother. What could Nina say other than she was glad the woman lived in Kentucky. Not too far to drive for holiday visits. Not so close that she would come over every week to inspect their house.

Charles, Nina and Donavan were in the dinning room, sitting down for tea with the formidable Mildred Douglas. The room was spectacular. A crystal chandelier hung above the 72-inch walnut colored double pedestal dining table. The china cabinet had porcelain figurines and formal china plates that Nina hadn't even dreamed of owning inside of it. The upholstered chairs were so cushiony soft that Nina melted into the seat.

"My son is a man of quality. It'll take a special woman to capture his heart," Mrs. Douglas told Nina, as if Charles's love for her was still up for debate.

Nervously, Charles grabbed Nina's hand and pulled her close. "Mama, a special woman has already captured my heart."

"You're forty, aren't you, dear?" Charles's mother asked Nina with a lift of her eyebrow.

"Thirty-six," Nina corrected.

"Don't you think that's a little old to start a family? You do know that Junior wants to have children?"

Charles came from a well-to-do family. Three generations of attorneys. But it was Charles II that turned the family into the yuppies they wanted to be. He made his bones on a triple homicide case. His wealthy client, whom everybody but his mama knew was guilty as sin, walked away scott free—well, not exactly free. Charles II charged that slasher three million dollars for his get-out-of-jail-for-everything-you've-got card.

Nina understood. She really did. This woman was just trying to preserve her way of life. She had grown accustomed to having everything the way she wanted it. Used to her children excelling. While Charles was a lawyer, his brothers and sisters were doctors, accountants, politicians. His baby sister was the CEO of a baby food company. Charles's sister couldn't just have five children, she had to go and invent the mushed up food the kids ate; bottle it and sell it to the tune of two million a year.

"Charles and I have discussed children," Nina told the woman with the most pleasant tone she could muster.

That got Donavan's attention. Questioning eyes turned toward his mother. Nina reached over and rubbed his arm reassuringly. Her eyes implored him to understand. He turned away.

By the time they left the Douglas home, Nina was a little bruised. Charles tried to talk her down from the ledge. "My mother is not a bad person, Nina. She'll warm up to you after we're married."

Nina looked at him skeptically.

He squeezed her hand. "You'll see." Charles's expression changed, darkened. "I wouldn't have let you meet with her so soon, but it couldn't be helped."

Nina turned toward him. Something in his voice sounded like trouble to her. "What's going on, Charles?"

He shut his eyes. Bad decision, since they were on I-71. The car swerved, he opened his eyes and steadied it. "Sorry about that."

Donavan sat up in the backseat. "Man, where'd you learn to drive? Kmart?"

"Sit back, Donavan," Nina scolded.

"I told you about this case I'm working on, right?" Charles moved them back to the subject at hand.

"That Mickey Jones guy?" Nina asked.

Donavan sat back in his seat and looked out the window, ears perked up to listen to Charles and his mother.

"Yeah. Well, anyway, that animal has started threatening my family. I don't want you or Donavan to get hurt. That's why I took you to see my mother now." He tried to smile, but his heart wasn't in it. "I don't think I should be around the two of you until I can get this case under wraps."

Nina looked worried. "So, do you want to call off the wedding?"

"No, no." Charles shook his head. "Nothing like that. Let's set the date, but you'll have to do the planning on your own. Let me put this guy away, then I won't feel so exposed."

"But you *do* still want to marry me?"

He put his hand over hers. "Of course, baby. I just don't want to put you in harm's way." He lifted her hand and kissed it. "To make matters worse, word on the street is— some young punks robbed one of Mickey's crack houses."

Donavan's head snapped around like Linda Blair in *The Exorcist*. He leaned in closer.

"Serves him right," Nina said. "He's out here selling his poison to these kids, someone should rob him."

"Only problem is, Mickey is one twisted drug dealer. He's not normal, Nina. I just hope we put him in jail before he finds those idiots who robbed him."

They drove in silence, listening to the radio. When Charles pulled the car up to Nina's house he turned toward Donavan. "Sorry, I won't be able to celebrate your birthday with you."

Donavan scooted out of the car. "Don't worry about it. I might not be celebrating it either."

# 16

Mickey stormed through his house like the mad hatter. Laquita cautiously walked behind him, being careful to stay out of his way.

"That lousy DA thinks he's so smart. Thinks he's going to get to me," Mickey mumbled while slinging the freezer door open. He threw a couple of the frozen entrees around, then turned on Laquita.

"I thought I told you to get me some more Freeze Pops?"

The kitchen island was between them. Laquita clutched the edge of it. "You mentioned them, but I thought you were going to pick them up. I'll go to the store right now if you want me to."

"Forget it." He slammed the freezer door." You can't do nothing right. I don't know why I bother with you."

He stared her down. Laquita lowered her head. She was pretty. Pouty lips and cocoa skin. Her hair was long, just the way he liked it. He often wrapped it around his hand and yanked. Pretty enough to model, but she was too stupid to put on the three-inch heels and walk down a runway. She'd rather be a dope man's woman. "I should have figured out that you wasn't worth two dead flies when your own mama threw your tired behind in the street. But me and my generous heart had to go pick you up, put food in your stomach and give you a decent place to stay."

Silence. Head still bowed low.

He turned away from her, shaking his head. "I got the Feds on my back, some suckas done robbed me, and I can't even get a Freeze Pop in my own house." He kicked up his feet on the coffee table in the living room and hollered back to Laquita, "Fix me a sandwich. Do something to earn your keep."

He picked up the phone and dialed Lou. He and Lou went way back. They started in the drug game together, but Isaac always thought Lou was small time. To this day, Lou was still proving Isaac right. From time to time, Mickey called on him though. He commissioned him as sort of a researcher. The project Lou was currently researching had to do with the robbery of one of Mickey's crack houses. "Found out anything yet?"

Mickey wanted to laugh. He could hear Lou flipping pages. Everywhere the boy went, he carried this small note pad. Nobody could tell him he wasn't a real detective. "Hey, Lou," he wanted to scream, "detectives don't get paid in crack." But in truth, Mickey had to give Lou his props. The boy could find Bin Laden if the price was right.

"Nothing yet, boss," Lou reported.

"Don't play me, Lou. Nothing goes on in the streets that you don't know about."

"I'm working on it. I'll have your information. Just give me a little more time."

His feet came off the table just as Laquita walked in with a man size turkey sandwich on toasted bread. "Get me my information, Lou. Don't play me after I've given you my merchandise."

"I wouldn't play you, Mickey. Honest, I'll have something on this in a couple of days."

"Tomorrow," Mickey screamed. "Or this will be your last case. You got me?" He slammed down the phone and looked at his pathetic woman. Leaning back against the couch he told her, "Feed me."

When she bent down to pick up the sandwich, he sat up and grabbed a fist full of her hair. The gold in his gleaming mouth greeted her as she shifted to face him.

"Mickey, if I did something wrong, just tell me. I can fix it," Laquita told him as worry lines etched her face.

He yanked her hair, pulling her closer. He was still smiling when he back handed Laquita and sent her tumbling to the floor. He really liked those Freeze Pops, especially the orange ones. He bent over her, pinning her arms to the ground with his knees. Slapping and punching. Slapping and punching.

"I'm sorry, Mickey. I w-won't do it again," she cried.

She lost consciousness somewhere between the fifteenth and the twentieth blow. When she came to, she was lying on the kitchen floor. Her vision was blurry, but she could see Mickey. He was standing over her again. A baseball bat in one hand, a rope in the other. That's when things started to go bad for Laquita.

# 17

Isaac picked up Donavan early Saturday morning and brought him back to West Virginia with him. Isaac knew that he would have a busy week at Faith Temple beginning Monday, but he wanted to spend a little time with his son before the drama began.

Donavan was subdued, and seemed content to sit in a corner and watch Isaac study his Word and write the sermon for Sunday. He didn't want to go anywhere. Isaac thought that was odd, but decided not to make a big deal about it, since he wanted to make this sermon one of the best he'd ever delivered anyway. "Help me, Lord."

He drove Donavan home early Tuesday morning. He missed school on Monday, but Donavan didn't seem to mind. Nina was another story. She looked at Isaac with scolding eyes, kind of like how she normally looked at Donavan. He ignored her and turned to his son.

"Hugs, not drugs," he wanted to say as he squeezed his son against him. "I love you, boy. I know I've been preoccupied lately, but I'm going to make this up to you. Okay?"

Donavan squeezed his father right back. "Thanks for coming to get me, Dad. I'm sorry for how I've been acting too." Donavan's eyes were moist when they parted. He opened his mouth to speak further, then decided against it.

Isaac caught a glimpse of something. He wasn't sure what, but something was wrong. His son was probably hating this whole wedding thing as much as he was. "If something's bothering you, you know you can talk to me, don't you?"

"Yeah." He bowed his head and wiped his eyes. "I'm okay, Dad." He brushed by him. "I've got to get ready for school."

"I'm going to drop you off. Let me know when you're ready," Nina hollered after Donavan as he walked into the house.

Isaac looked at his watch. "Didn't I get him here in time enough to catch his bus?"

Nina leaned in closer to Isaac and whispered. "He's been skipping school. The secretary from the Attendance Office called me on Friday."

Isaac's fingers rubbed upward, past his forehead, through his wavy hair. "Okay, something's going on, and we need to get to the bottom of it." He looked at Nina, trying to avoid that blasted ring. "Look, when I get finished with this situation in West Virginia, the two of us need to sit down with Donavan and make him talk to us." Nina agreed, then Isaac reluctantly got back on the road.

The police had arrested Pastor Marks yesterday. Several members of the church resigned their membership. Other members had called the church demanding to see Bishop. So, Isaac and Bishop's calendar would be full for the rest of the week.

The church secretary had provided Isaac and Bishop Sumler with a list of all the members she knew for sure that Pastor Marks had known in the Biblical sense. They were going to contact these women, once Bishop installed a new pastor, and encourage them to continue attending Faith Temple.

The third woman through Isaac's door ranted and raved about how she knew Marks was no good. "Them little beady eyes of his was always staring at the ladies." She finished up by telling Isaac she didn't know how she could continue going to a church with such loose morals. Her name was on the list the secretary provided him with.

It was now noon, so Isaac took a lunch break and called Cassandra. She was as pleasant as ever. He enjoyed talking to her. A welcomed change from all the drama he was going through today.

"It looks like I won't be back in town until late Sunday night," he told her.

"Don't you worry about anything here. I've already tidied up your place. Oh, yeah, that reminds me. Boy, you are a slob."

Isaac laughed. It felt good to laugh. "Yeah, I know. I need a maid, just can't afford one."

"Well, don't be looking at me like some domestic. I'm just helping out in a time of need."

Leaning back in his seat, Isaac said, "Maybe I'll always need you."

"Don't make promises, Isaac. I just may hold you to them."

He liked the sound of that. He gripped the phone tighter and leaned in to do some low talking just as another disgruntled member of Faith Temple knocked on his door.

He sat up. "Look, Cassandra, I've got to get back to work. I'm going to take you out to dinner when I get back, so think about what you want to eat."

"Isaac, I'm a simple girl. You can take me over to Gino's and I'll be happy."

His kind of woman. These days anyway, when money was hard to come by. "I'll talk to you later."

Two days later, Isaac was on the phone with Cassandra and the words, "I miss you," fell out his mouth.

"I can't get you off my mind either, Isaac. I'm glad you'll be home soon."

Isaac smiled. It felt good to have somebody on his side. Maybe this would be the woman who could stand with him against the world. "Look here, Cassandra. When I get back home, I'm talking about spending some exclusive time with you. Are you dealing with anybody else that I should know about?"

"Nobody but you, baby," she said with a slight hint of contentment in her voice.

*Just what he wanted to hear.* The grin on his face couldn't get much bigger. If she had been sitting in front of him, he would have tapered it down a notch. Always got to be cool. "I'll see you in a couple days."

# 18

Donavan was no honor student, but when JC showed up on his doorstep early Sunday morning, he knew something had gone really wrong. He stepped out on his porch, closing the door softly. Looking up and down his block, like he was getting ready to cross the street or something, he asked, "Man, what you doing here?"

JC wasted little time in turning Donavan's bright day gray. "Baby Dee is dead."

Donavan stumbled, but regained his balance by grabbing hold of the banister. "What do you mean, Baby Dee is dead?"

JC jumped around the porch, slamming his fist into his open palm. "I mean that psychopath slit Baby Dee's throat and left him in the alley behind Anna Street."

Donavan would have given anything to be able to talk to his father. But what would he say? *"Hey, Dad, I robbed this mad man and now he's trying to kill me."* His dad would go ballistic. If Mickey didn't kill him, Isaac Walker would.

This was supposed to be a good time of year for him. School was almost out. Fun in the sun was approaching, and in two days, he would be twelve, or he would be dead. "Maybe we should give Mickey his money back."

"Are you crazy?" JC asked. "He'll know we robbed him if we give back the money."

Again, Donavan was no honor student, but the friction in his brain worked well enough to put two and two together. If Mickey killed Baby Dee, it's a sure bet that he already knew. "Maybe if we give him the money back, he'll leave us alone."

"Are you for real, Donavan? That lunatic would take that money out of our hands and slit our throats at the same time." JC shook his head. "Mickey ain't wrapped right. He's even got his mama on the street turning tricks."

Donavan wished someone would have explained how much of a lunatic Mickey was when they were planning to rob him. Turning his head to look up and down the street, and then up and down the street again he whispered, "Well, what do you think we should do?"

Nina came to the door and peeked out. "Donavan, you need to get back in here and get ready for church." She looked toward Donavan's visitor. "Oh, hi, JC. Are you planning to go to church with us this morning?"

"Uh-uh, no ma'am," JC said, shaking his head.

"Then you need to talk with Donavan some other time." Looking back to her son she added, "Two minutes."

"Okay, okay. I'm coming," he told her as she closed the front door.

JC jumped around the porch again. "I don't know, I just don't know what to do."

Reaching for the doorknob, Donavan told him, "When you figure something out, let me know."

JC grabbed his arm. "Where do you think you're going? We're in this together."

Donavan yanked his arm from JC's grasp. "Look, I've got

to get ready for church. Call me when you figure something out."

JC walked off the porch mumbling. "You go on to church, but let me tell you something, Shortie, if I go down, you'll come tumbling after me."

"Thanks for the pep talk, JC. I'll see you later." Donavan went inside and dressed for church faster than he had in his entire life. Church was where he needed to be. He wanted to lift his hands in praise. Today, he would listen to what the preacher had to say; but most of all, he was going to pray.

# 19

Praise and worship was a time of renewal. Hands lifted up to the Lord. "What a mighty God we serve," was shouted from the congregation, pulpit and balcony. "Angels bow before Him, heaven and earth adore Him."

Donavan's hands were lifted halfway, as if to say, "Uh-uh, I'm not surrendering to you, Lord. I've got too much life to live."

Nina knelt on the floor. This was her preferred position. It meant total surrender. She never understood how people could stand, hands half raised to a holy God. Her God was too awesome, too wondrous not to—well not to do what the next song called for, "I surrender all to thee, my blessed Savior. I surrender all."

Pastor McKinley tore the house up as usual. The man had a low tolerance for sin. He said that instead of just loving the things God loves, Christians should learn to hate what God hates. If saints hated sin as much as God does, then maybe they wouldn't fall into it so easily.

Nina loved her church. She had learned a lot about living for God from her pastor, but she still missed Marguerite. The woman had been so kind to her all those years ago, when Isaac beat her down behind an abortion clinic. She had considered aborting Donavan, but when she got to that God-awful place, she just couldn't go through with it. Thank God Isaac's beat down didn't cause her to miscarry. Marguerite had been so good to her back then. She took Nina into her home and brought her to church. Nina would always be grateful to Marguerite for her kindness. If only she was still alive, she'd know what to do about Donavan.

Nina glanced at her son. Normally, he was fidgety in service. He was one of those, is-it-over, is-it-over-yet, kinds of kids. But today, he was—she didn't know how to explain it, but it looked like he was paying attention to the sermon. The furrow in his brow told her he didn't seem to like what he was hearing, but he was listening. Then something really strange happened. Donavan bowed his head, and—and *prayed*. No words escaped his lips, so she couldn't avow to it, but the closed eyes and the hands against his forehead were a dead give away.

Nina didn't want to make a big deal of this. She should be glad that her son was praying, but her gut told her something was wrong. Something she missed, something she should have noticed.

Nina whispered, "Oh, Lord, please help me. I don't know what to do."

When they got home, she went to her bedroom, locked the door, and then called Isaac's cell. As mad as Isaac made her, she always called him when things got too complicated. That probably deserved some thought time, but not now. The phone rang twice, then Isaac picked up.

"Hey, do you have a minute?" she asked him.

Isaac rubbed his eyes and yawned. "Yeah, what's up?"

"I'm sorry, Isaac. I didn't think you would be sleep. I can call you later."

"No. Don't worry about it."

Nina could hear the rustle of Isaac's sheets as he shifted himself around.

"I was just catching a quick nap before getting on the road." He yawned again. "I need to get up anyway. I delivered my last sermon in West Virginia this morning and I'm ready to go home."

She wanted him to stop in Dayton on his way home. She would feel much better if he was there right now, but she could hear how tired he was. She wouldn't push. Just let him know the situation. "I think something's going on with Donavan."

"You already told me that he's been skipping school."

She raised her hand as if he could see the motion. "Not just the school thing. He was praying today."

Isaac laughed. "I don't think that's such a bad thing."

"Trust me on this, Isaac. Something's going on." She stood and paced the room. Her voice quivered when she added, "I feel it in my gut."

"Okay, Nina, calm down. Instead of waiting until next weekend to talk with Donavan, why don't we do it on Tuesday?"

"Donavan's birthday is on Tuesday."

"Exactly. We'll take him to dinner, maybe a movie, then we'll sit down and talk this out."

Nina relaxed a bit. "Okay, I guess it can wait 'til Tuesday."

They finished making birthday plans, then hung up. Nina was getting ready to leave her bedroom when the phone rang again. She leaped on it, thinking maybe Isaac had changed his mind. Maybe he was going to stop in Dayton on his way home.

"Hey, baby. Are you missing me as much as I'm missing you?"

"Charles?" Nina hadn't missed him. She hadn't had time to think about Charles for worrying about Donavan. Once she could get this thing with Donavan out of the way, she'd have more time to focus on her future husband. "I've been so busy, I haven't even noticed that you weren't around." She said it playfully, but it was the truth. That bothered her. It also bothered her that she was okay with Charles not participating in Donavan's birthday celebration. Another point to ponder.

"Ha ha, you're just too funny. Anyway, I called to tell you that I might be able to come over on Tuesday for Donavan's birthday."

Her eyes bucked, panic caused her heart to race. Isaac and Charles in the same room? "B-but I thought you said we wouldn't be able to see each other for awhile."

"That was before that animal beat his girlfriend bloody, black and blue."

Her hand covered her mouth as she gasped. "Oh, my God."

"Oh, my God is right, Nina. This girl might not make it through the night. I don't even want to tell you all that animal did to her." He sighed. "At least the judge won't approve bail when he gets arrested this time."

When Nina hung up the phone, she put her problems on the back burner and prayed for the battered girl Charles told her about. If nothing else, Nina knew that prayer could change things. So, she prayed that the girl would live, be healthy, give her life to Christ and leave the Mickeys of this world alone for good. She prayed all of that in Jesus' mighty name.

Blurry vision was bad, real bad on the highway. Coffee. Isaac hated the aftertaste, but if it would keep him alive, he'd endure it. While pumping himself full of caffeine in the gas station/restaurant, Isaac saw a little boy who looked a lot like Donavan. His mom was petite with short hair like Nina's. But the guy who grabbed hold of the boy's hand looked nothing like him. He was always the odd man out lately. No wonder his son was having problems.

It was about nine o'clock in the evening when he got back on the road. He picked up the phone to check on his son.

Donavan answered on the first ring. "Hello."

He didn't sound right to Isaac. Almost as if he were scared. Real scared. "You all right, son?"

"Oh, Dad. It's you."

"Yeah, it's me. You don't sound right. What's going on with you?"

"Nothing, Dad. I'm just tired."

"Boy, you're eleven years old. You don't have no business being tired."

"Almost twelve," Donavan said proudly.

Isaac smiled. "Yeah, Tuesday's the big day for you. So what do you want for your birthday?"

After an uncomfortable pause, Donavan replied, "I just want you to be here. Can you come, Dad?"

"I wouldn't miss it for the world."

"Not even for your ministry obligations?"

He heard the doubt in his son's voice and wanted to kick himself for it. "I've already worked out the details with your mother. We're going to take you out to dinner. I'll be there. Count on it."

"Okay, Dad. I can't wait to see you."

Isaac was smiling when they hung up. His son sounded excited about seeing him again. Maybe their weekend together had done more good than he thought.

Before he could lay his phone down, Cassandra rang in. "You got me on your mind, huh?" Isaac joked with her.

"You know I do. When will you be home?"

"I've got a couple more hours on the road, but I should make it in a little before midnight."

"Well, everything is in tip-top shape at your house. You should be able to fall right into bed and not worry about a thing."

His back was aching from the long drive. As much as he

hated to admit it, he was getting older. Needed more rest these days. "That sounds good."

"Oh, and I've got a surprise for you."

His cell phone chirped at him. Low battery.

"Cassandra, can you hear me?"

"Yes, I can hear you."

"My phone is about to die on me." He always forgot to charge the stupid thing. He didn't have a car charger with him. "So, tell me quick. What's the surprise?"

Her voice was low and seductive as she said, "Well, I think you will enjoy—"

"Cassandra, Cassandra," Isaac called out her name, but it was no use. The battery was dead.

# 20

Donavan hung up the phone, wishing that his father was with him right now. When his dad asked what he wanted for his birthday, he almost told him that he wanted to be alive. But to tell his father that, he'd have to admit to skipping school to help his friends rob a crack house. No, he wasn't going there. Not with Isaac Walker.

Pacing around his room, Donavan wondered how in the world he'd gotten into the mess he was in. And more importantly, how he would get out? Why wasn't he like normal kids? Why'd he have to skip school and join up with a bunch of hoodlums? The more he thought about it, the dumber he felt. His mom and dad had cautioned him against hanging around losers. So, what had he done? Picked JC, king of the losers, as a friend.

"You really need to work on your decision making skills," he told himself.

He pulled the shoebox from under his bed and counted the three hundred dollars again. He pounded his forehead with his palm. "You are so stupid." He was going to get his throat slit for a lousy three hundred dollars. He kept telling himself that it just didn't seem worth it. But he was a stupid kid who thought being mad at his mother and father gave him license to do whatever he pleased. The worst part about this whole thing was that Donavan no longer wanted to run away, so he no longer needed a stash of money.

He was sliding the box back under his bed when JC rung his phone.

"Okay, Shortie, Let's do it," JC said. He sounded excited.

Donavan's brows furrowed, "Let's do what?"

"You know. What you said."

The conversation reminded Donavan of that commercial where the camera panned the ground and the announcer said, "*This is your brain.*" Then they cracked an egg on the hot summer ground, and told all the crack heads of America, "*This is your brain on drugs.*"

"JC, what are you talking about?

"I called Mickey. Told him I was giving back his money like you suggested."

"I don't think I suggested that you call him up. I was thinking that we'd leave the money on his door step with a note or something."

"Naw, it's cool. It's cool. Mickey said just bring him the money and all will be forgiven."

Donavan didn't say anything, he was too busy mulling over the news and wondering if Mickey could be trusted to keep his word.

"Did you spend any of the money I gave you?" JC asked Donavan.

"No, I still have it all."

"Oh, man. You don't know how happy I am to hear that. Look, I told Mickey that I would meet him at Broadway Park behind the shelter at eleven tonight. Can you meet me over there at about quarter 'til?"

Nothing would make Donavan happier than to give back the blood money. He looked at the clock on his dresser. It was almost ten o'clock. "I'll be there."

He went downstairs to check on his mother. Nina was in the family room, sitting on the sofa reading her Bible. Donavan knew what would come next. She would be knelt down, if not sprawled out, on the floor praying. "What book of the Bible are you reading tonight?" Donavan asked. Nina had told him so many of the stories from the Bible that Donavan felt as if he knew King David and Apostle Paul personally.

Nina looked up and smiled at her son. "I thought you were in bed."

"Couldn't sleep."

"Do you want to talk?" Nina asked as she moved the Bible from her lap and sat it on the table in order to give Donavan her full attention.

"No. What for?" he said defensively.

"Oh, well. Do you want to watch a movie together?"

He really did want to watch a movie with his mom, but he had to get a stalker off his back first. "Not right now. I don't want to stop you from spending time with God. So, tell me, what are you reading about?"

She glanced toward her Bible. "I'm in First Samuel. There's a story about a woman who couldn't have children. Well, one day she went to the house of God and cried out to Him. She told God that if He would give her a child, she would give the child back to Him.

"God granted her request. So, after she had baby Samuel, she took him back to the church and left him with the priest. Samuel served God all the days of his life."

Donavan's brows lifted. "What was the point of having the child if she was going to give it away?"

Nina laughed. "I'm sure it was hard for her. But you know what I think, Donavan?"

"Nope, but I know you're going to tell me."

She playfully hit him on the arm. "I think this story was put in the Bible to teach us the importance of dedicating our children to the Lord."

"Did you dedicate me to God?"

"I sure did. And I've prayed for you ever since."

"I hate to break it to you, Mom, but I'm no Samuel."

Nina stood and hugged her son. "Your latter will be greater than your beginning, Donavan." She stepped back and looked at the young man in front of her. "You will do great things for God. I know that like I know my own name."

Donavan thought about the watch his dad had given him inscribed with: GOD IS GREAT IN YOU. The same watch that he almost lost to a drug dealer. "Are you sure that you and Dad aren't just wishing this stuff? Maybe God doesn't want somebody like me."

With a determined look in her eyes she told him, "You are a man of God." Grabbing his shoulders, Nina continued, "You will fulfill the call of God on your life."

He shook his head as he walked away. He was a heathen, and his sainted mother couldn't see it. How could he be a man of God when he was a thief on his way to give the dope man back his money? Yeah, he could just see God sitting on His throne high-fiving Jesus over the mighty exploits of Donavan Walker.

# 21

He was as quiet as possible while climbing out his bedroom window. Donavan didn't normally sneak out until his mom was good and sleep. Right now, she was speaking in tongues and calling on the Lord. He hoped like crazy that she was praying for him.

"Let me get this done, Lord, and this will be the last time I sneak out of the house for anything."

His pockets were fat with money that belonged to Mickey, the crazed lunatic, as he rounded the corner. On Broadway, with the park in clear view, he didn't like what he saw. The park was dark and deserted. Somebody was always up there shooting hoops.

"Oh, Lord. I'd sure like this to turn out okay," he said as he inched closer to his destination. Maybe he should speak in tongues like his mother. Maybe God would hear his pleas then.

Standing in front of the park, Donavan wished he knew how to speak in tongues. He really wanted to try some of that I-tie-my-bow-tie-honda-my-mama stuff. The streetlights were busted. Wouldn't nobody be able to see over by the shelter with the lights out. Slowly, he walked toward the destination. "JC," he called out.

No answer.

"JC, are you back there?" He picked up a couple of rocks and peeked his head around the corner. What he saw caused him to shake. He felt something warm going down his leg.

"Get on around here, bad little nigga."

That comment came from Mickey. He was holding a razor, JC's seven foot form was stretched out on the ground, throat slit.

Donavan's legs carried him forward even though his brain screamed for him to backtrack all the way home. "What did you do to him?" Donavan screamed at Mickey.

Mickey smirked. "What did you do in your pants?"

Donavan looked down. To his mortification, his jeans were wet all the way down to his shoes.

"Looks like somebody's afraid of the boogie man," Mickey taunted.

"Why'd you have to kill him? He was going to give you the money." Donavan pulled his portion of the ill-gotten gain from his pocket and threw it at Mickey.

"Now see, why'd you have to throw my money like it's trash or something? You better be glad that I go way back with your dad." Mickey gave Donavan a stare down, then pointed at his cash on the ground. "Pick it up."

"You crazy. I'm not bending down to give you easy access to *my* throat."

"I don't like the fact that you don't trust me. I told you I go way back with your daddy." He folded the razor and put it in his pocket. "I have another punishment for you."

"Yeah, what?" He might have peed his pants, but he wasn't about to sound like no little girl.

"Get on your knees. Beg my forgiveness and then I'll tell you what your fate will be."

"Forget that. I'm not kneeling down so you can slit my

throat. If you're going to do me, I'll be standing." He pulled the rocks from behind his back and threw them at Mickey. They slammed into Mickey's face. Blood gushed from his nose and cheek. Donavan turned and kicked up dust. What is it they say? A good run was better than a bad stand? If Mickey was going to slit his throat, Donavan was going to be a straight punk about it. *Catch me if you can, psycho.*

While Donavan was running, screaming, "Help. Help," a song came to mind. "If I ever needed the Lord, sure do need Him now, right now." He'd always liked that song. His mom hummed it around the house and nothing bad ever happened to her. When he took a break from the "Help. Help" song, he sang, "Sure do need you now, right now."

Mickey wiped the blood from his face and licked it. He laughed. "If that boy isn't just like his daddy, I don't know who is."

He almost hated to kill him. After all, Isaac had been his mentor. He had looked out for him. Walking over to his car, he chided himself, "Don't do this, Mickey. Cut the kid a break. Do it for Isaac."

But hadn't he bought Isaac a nice Lincoln truck when he'd been released from prison? Isaac didn't want it. Even bought Isaac a house and was going to throw Isaac some cash so he wouldn't have to come home and grind from scratch. But Isaac didn't want that either. Mickey was confused. He couldn't predict what Isaac wanted anymore. So who was he to say that Isaac wouldn't want him to gut the life out of his thieving little son?

He jumped in his car with purpose. The night stalker was back in business. He turned the radio up as he gassed the peddle. A popular release from 50 Cent was in his CD player, blasting ignorance. "Many men wish death upon me."

Mickey's head bobbed back and forth as he reached in the glove compartment and grabbed his gun. He turned on Donavan's street. Run, Forest, run. That little knucklehead could have been the next Carl Lewis. Look at him go.

Nina was on the porch waiting for Donavan when he bounded up the stairs. She stood and snatched him up. "Boy, where have you been?" Donavan was panting, looking around like somebody was chasing him. "What have you gotten yourself into?"

"Not now, Mama. Let's go in the house." He tried to move her toward the door, but she wasn't budging.

"This is the perfect time." Her finger was in his face. "I know what you've been doing."

Donavan's eyes widened.

Walking the length of the porch, arms going every which way but loose, she told him, "You've been skipping school. And now, now I catch you sneaking out of the house."

Donavan watched the Lincoln inch toward them. He didn't want to be responsible for anything happening to his mother. He tried to push her down.

Nina stumbled but quickly regained her balance. "You've gone too far now, Donavan."

She grabbed hold of her son and shook him. "Come with me, I'm calling your father."

"No!" Donavan screamed and pulled away from Nina while trying to push her down again.

Mickey saw Nina. Whew, she was good and mad. Arms flailing in the air—giving that prodigal a piece of her mind. 'Bout time.

He rolled down the window and leaned over. He almost wanted to wait, see if that knucklehead would finally get the beating he's been begging for. Donavan turned and looked at him. His eyes went wild as he tried to push his mother out of the way. She was pretty tough though.

Watch out. Here comes the night stalker.

"Donavan, what are you doing?" she screamed at him, refusing to budge.

"Get down, Mama! Get down!"

The first bullet hit Donavan in the back. Nina grabbed her son and moved him behind her. Mickey heard her say, "Lord, Jesus help us," as he lit her, Donavan and the porch up with the rest of the bullets in his clip.

Her body seemed to lift off the ground with the assault of the bullets. She floated down, kind of angelic like.

"Wow." Mickey had never seen anything so beautiful. He wished he had a camera. He'd call the shot, 'The Floating Dead.' He drove away wishing he could do it again.

# Part Two

O Lord, you have searched me and know me.
You know my sitting down and my rising up; you
understand my thoughts afar off.
You comprehend my path and my lying down, and are
acquainted with all my ways.
For there is not a word on my tongue, but behold
O Lord, you know it altogether.
You have hedged me behind and before, and laid your hand
upon me.
Such knowledge is too wonderful for me; it is high, I
cannot attain it.
Where can I go from your Spirit? Or where can I flee from
your presence?
If I ascend into heaven, you are there; if I make my bed
in hell, behold, you are there.

*Psalm 139: 1-8*

## 22

Isaac raced into the emergency room at Grand View Hospital. Eyes darting to and fro, searching out someone, anyone with answers. A nurse tried to walk past him. Isaac grabbed her arm. "Do you know anything about my son—his mother?"

"Excuse me?" she asked while retrieving her arm from his grasp.

His eyes were wild. Thrusting his hand through his hair he tried again. "My son and his mother were shot last night. Nina Lewis and Donavan Walker."

"Oh, yes." She pointed to an open door to the left of the emergency room. "You might want to wait in there with the rest of the family. Dr. Hamilton and Dr. Kym have just finished surgery. They'll be in to see you in just a moment."

*What family? He was their only family.*

Walking into the small room, Isaac was greeted by Michael and Char Edwards. Michael was an elder at Nina's church and the brother of Nina's best friend, Elizabeth Underwood.

"Isaac, thank God you made it," Elder Edwards said while clasping a hand to his shoulder.

"What happened, Mike?" Isaac asked.

He squeezed Isaac's shoulder. "We only have bits and pieces of what happened. Donavan was running home. Before he could get in the house Nina stopped him and was yelling at him. The next thing the neighbors knew, some guy started shooting at them."

"It's all my fault. Oh, God. It's all my fault," Charles said.

Isaac turned to see Charles Douglas seated in one of the leather chairs in the center of the room. His hands were over his bowed head. Brushing Elder Edwards's hand from his shoulder, Isaac stalked over to Charles. "What do you mean, this is all your fault?"

Keith walked into the small room and tossed the keys to Isaac. "The car is on the second floor in the garage."

Isaac grabbed his keys then turned back to Charles. A look of unmistakable misery covered Charles's face. Isaac pulled him out of the chair by his collar. "What did you do?"

Keith and Michael grabbed Isaac and pulled him away. "Come on, man. Don't do this in here," Keith begged.

"What did you do?" Isaac demanded of Charles while trying to get free.

Crumpling back in his seat, Charles cried out. "Oh, God, why?"

"Charles thinks this young punk he's prosecuting shot Nina and Donavan," Michael replied as he and Keith released Isaac.

Isaac sat down. He expelled an exasperated breath. "Why would this guy want to kill Nina and Donavan?"

Desperately, Charles tried to pull himself together. He wiped his eyes and calmed himself as he told the group, "Mickey Jones is a sick little criminal who needs the electric chair. He's been sending me death threats since the hearing." Charles lifted his hands to God and rolled his eyes upward while shaking his head. "I stopped going by Nina's house so they would be safe from that animal."

If Isaac wasn't sitting, he would have fallen down. Charles was accusing *Mickey* of this brutal attack. *His* Mickey, from way back when? No way was something like this possible. No way Mickey would destroy his family.

Keith and Isaac's eyes locked. Silently, they were both saying, no way. It couldn't happen. Not in a million years would Mickey Jones do something like this to Isaac.

Leaning forward, Isaac told Charles, "I think you're wrong on this one, Counselor. Mickey didn't do this."

"Do you know him?"

"Yeah," Isaac answered defensively. "And the Mickey I know wouldn't do nothing like this."

"Really?" Charles stood and grabbed the file he'd left on the table. "I suppose the Mickey you know wouldn't do anything like this either, huh?" He showed Isaac pictures of a bruised and battered woman lying in a hospital bed. "He beat her with a bat. We've got a warrant out for his arrest, but we haven't found him yet."

Isaac's insides turned. He thought of the day Mickey met him outside the prison. When he got released from prison, the last thing he wanted to do was run into a hustler. But Mickey was there anyway.

Isaac remembered the look of desperation in Mickey's eyes. He remembered thinking that Mickey needed his help. But Isaac wanted nothing to do with the world he'd come from. The day he chose to leave with Bishop Sumler, he also chose to leave his past behind. Or had he? Was it his refusal to deal with Mickey's pain that brought tragedy to his doorstep five years later?

Dr. Hamilton stepped into the waiting room and stifled Isaac's pondering. "Okay, who is the next of kin?"

Isaac and Charles both stood.

Dr. Hamilton looked to Charles first. "How are you re-lated?"

"She's my fiancé."

"And you," he asked Isaac.

"Donavan is my son and Nina will be my wife."

Charles let out a frustrated blow and rolled his eyes. Isaac ignored him. "Look, Doc, can you tell us something? What's going on?"

"I just completed surgery on Nina Lewis. She had two abdominal wounds and one shoulder wound. She'll be laid up for quite awhile, but she'll survive."

Shouts and cheers of relief swept through the room. Isaac turned back to Dr. Hamilton. "What else?"

"What do you mean?"

Isaac stared him down. "I see it on your face. There's something you're not telling us."

Dr. Hamilton shook his head. "There is more, but I need to discuss it with my patient first. Alright?"

"Alright, Doc. What about my son?"

Dr. Kym had impeccable timing. No good news, but impeccable timing nonetheless. Walking in the room just as Isaac asked about Donavan, he said, "Well, I pulled two bullets out of the young man. I can't tell you anymore than that right now. If he lives through the night—"

"What are you talking about?" Isaac yelled at the doctor.

Dr. Kym lifted his hand. "Sir, I'm sorry, but the boy is very weak."

"Can I see my son?"

"We've got him hooked up to a respirator. He's not looking very go—"

Dr. Hamilton put his hand on Dr. Kym's shoulder. "Let the man see his son, Kym."

"Follow me," Dr. Kym told Isaac.

The angels in heaven stood betwixt and between. Swords drawn, waiting on God to release them for battle. Demonic forces were waging war against Isaac and his family. He had withstood blow after blow, but Isaac's resolve was weakening.

Davison, Isaac's angel, had walked through the fire with Isaac for seven years now; since the day he first bowed his knee to God in prison. He'd helped him get through trial after trial. But his charge was getting weary. "Come on, Isaac; pray!"

Pacing the streets of gold in the outer court, Davison was spooling for a fight. Knocking some demon heads together would make him feel a lot better. This thing has gone on far too long. His charge had been under attack from the moment he bowed his knees to Jesus. The demonic spirits of lust, anger and unforgiveness constantly plagued him.

Aaron, the captain of the angels, put his hand on Davison's shoulder. "Be patient. The saints of God will start praying."

Davison shook his head. "He can't take much more, Captain. These attacks have been too constant in his life."

"He's come too far. He will not forsake the Lord," Aaron assured him.

A look of uncertainty crossed Davison's face. "What if Donavan does not make it?"

"The saints will pray. The almighty God will make a way. His will be done." Aaron patted Davison's shoulder and walked away.

# 23

Rage.
Maddening fury.

Isaac's fists clenched, jaws tightened, as he stood over his son. His only son was in a coma. Tubes were everywhere. His son couldn't breathe on his own. The respirator was pumping life into him. Without it, Donavan would . . .

"Don't you die on me," Isaac commanded. "Do you hear me, Donavan? Don't you give up!"

Flashbacks of being in hell and seeing his son tortured assaulted his being. He picked up Donavan's hand and lightly squeezed it. "You're not going to open your eyes in hell, Donavan. I won't allow it." A bold declaration for one who, at that moment, refused to pray.

He'd brought his Bible to read to his son, but he wasn't going to do that. Not after seeing the shape his son was in. He was mad at God. Mad at Jesus. Mad at the twelve elders who bowed before the throne, distracting God. Mad at the four beasts who cried holy, holy, holy! Mad at the angels who obviously couldn't fight, nor protect nobody worth spit.

Slamming his Bible on the nightstand next to his son's

bed, Isaac remembered the doctor's words: "*If he lives through the night.*"

He put his hands to the side of his head to stop the violent shaking. He couldn't take much more. "Lord, I'm about to lose my mind."

He snuck down the hall to check on Nina. She seemed to be sleeping peacefully. Her arm was in a sling. He walked over to the bed and touched her bruised and puffy face. She was still beautiful to him. Still meant the world to him. He shoved his fist in his mouth to keep from yelling out.

His family had been attacked in the worst way, and he was supposed to stand around praying, waiting, and hoping? Forget that. He had prayed that his family would never come against tragedy, but tragedy had come.

Rubbing his chin, Isaac pondered this nightmare while walking back to Donavan's room. They still had a good seven hours worth of daylight before nightfall. His son was a fighter, a survivor. Today, Isaac would sit here and watch his son fight for his life. Tomorrow, he would find out exactly who was tired of living.


"Isaac, some guy out here wants to talk with you. He looks pretty shook up," Keith told him.

Isaac almost told Keith to send him away. He'd slept in the chair next to Donavan's bed. His back ached, shoulders needed a good rub down. One close call happened with the monitor going flat, but Donavan made it through the night.

He didn't want to be disturbed. He wanted coffee, and lots of it. But something in his gut nudged him forward. "Where is he?"

"He's in the waiting room."

Elizabeth Underwood was also in the waiting room when Isaac walked in. Elizabeth ran to him and embraced him. "How are you holding up?" she whispered in his ear.

He embraced her back. "Not too good."

"Yeah, I know." She softly rubbed his back, then they released each other.

"Never thought I'd be here for them," Isaac added.

The young man seated in the back of the room stood up. He held out his hand for Isaac. Isaac stared at it. "I-I'm Mark Smith. I'm a friend of your son's."

"Aren't you a little old to hang around Donavan?"

Mark smiled. "Actually, I'm a friend of JC's, or at least I used to be. Donavan hung around JC. That's how we met."

Isaac wanted him to cut to the chase already. "What can I do for you?"

Mark looked over at Charles and then back to Isaac. "Can we talk in private?"

He told Elizabeth that he would talk to her later, then turned back to Mark. "Come on out here." Isaac walked into an empty room on the opposite side of their waiting area. "What's up?"

Mark wrung his hands. "Sir, I'm real sorry for what happened to Donavan, but I think I know who did it."

"How would you know that?"

" 'Cause it has to be the same guy that killed Baby Dee and JC. According to JC, some dude named Lou ratted us out to Mickey Jones."

Again, someone was accusing Mickey. Isaac's stomach turned, like it did when he was ten years old and his grandmother had told him five of the neighborhood kids came to her complaining about Isaac taking their lunch money— "*Everybody ain't gon' tell the same lie,*" his grandmother had said when Isaac denied bullying the kids. Mickey was guilty.

"Why do you think Mickey did this?"

" 'Cause the four of us robbed him a couple weeks ago."

Isaac's brow went up. "The four of who?"

"JC, Baby Dee, Donavan and myself. We robbed one of Mickey's crack houses. Word on the street was, he didn't take it so well."

"I told Donavan not to hang around that JC. I knew nothing good would come out of it. Looking at the boy's mama and daddy, a fool could see that JC wasn't gon' be nothing." Balling his fist, Isaac pounded on the wall. What was Donavan thinking? What would an eleven-year-old need with money so bad he'd steal to get it? But even as he asked the question, he remembered stealing from a grocery store when he was Donavan's age. "Why does it always come back around?" he asked the walls, wind, and air. No one answered. He turned back on Mark. "How did you manage to stay alive?"

"I went back to college. You know, got out of Dodge," Mark told him before grief covered his face. "But JC was my best friend. We go way back."

Isaac shook his head. "Why would grown men use a kid to rob somebody?"

Again Mark said, "Sir, I'm sorry. I should have never gone to JC with my financial problems. Now my best friend is dead and your son is fighting for his life." Mark slumped down in the chair against the wall and cried out. "Oh, God, forgive me. Please."

Isaac turned cold eyes on Mark. God had better forgive him, 'cause he never would. Isaac wasn't about to forgive Mickey or JC's hell rotting behind either. Storming out of the room, Isaac had but one thought on his mind. Find Mickey and make him pay.

"Hey, where are you going?" Keith asked when he saw Isaac heading down the corridor.

"I've got some business to take care of. I'll be back."

Keith caught up with him. "Pastor McKinley is on his way back out here. We're going to have a prayer vigil for Nina and Donavan."

Was Keith crazy? Had he lost his mind? Isaac's woman—

or at least she should have been his woman—and son were laid up in the hospital because somebody he had once fed shot them. And they wanted to pray. He wasn't taking this one on bended knee. "You go pray. I've got things to do."

Keith grabbed his friend's shoulder. "I know that look, Isaac. Don't do this."

Isaac didn't answer.

"I'm coming with you."

Isaac punched the down button for the elevator. "I don't want you to miss your prayer meeting. I can handle my business alone."

"I'm going."

They rode in the car in silence. Keith praying, Isaac plotting. West Dayton hadn't changed much, except that now his son had been gunned down on its mean streets. Isaac had tried to leave the violence behind him. Tried to do the right thing. But just like Apostle Paul, whenever Isaac tried to do good, evil followed him. He didn't know how to shake it, and was tired of trying. The Godfather was right, every time you try to get out, some sucka pulls you back in.

By the time they pulled in front of Lou's shack, Isaac had turned like a dog back to his vomit. He banged on Lou's door like the rent man with an eviction notice. "I know you're in there, Lou. Don't make me knock this door down."

"Hold on. What's the emergency?" Lou said from within the house.

Keith stood back.

Lou opened the door and Isaac grabbed him by his throat. "You know what it is, and don't play me."

"Isaac, my man. It's good to see you," Lou said, the best he could with a hand clenching his throat.

Breathing mean, mad dog air in Lou's face, Isaac asked through clenched teeth, "Why didn't you tell me what was going on, Lou?"

"It's not my fault, Isaac. I didn't tell Mickey that Donavan had a part in the robbery. How was I supposed to know he'd find out?"

Isaac pushed Lou away from him. "Where is he?"

Lou shook his head. "He's gone crazy, Isaac. That boy thinks he's king of the hill around here. He's killing everything in sight."

"Where is he?" Isaac demanded, slamming Lou against the wall.

Lou raised his hands. "Calm down, man. The police have been looking for Mickey because of what he did to his girlfriend, so he's been moving from place to place. The last I heard, he was holding up in one of his crack houses."

Isaac released him again. "You still got my stuff?" Years ago, when Isaac got sent up, Lou went to his house and collected all his weapons. For safe keeping, he told Isaac.

"You know I do." He went into his basement and came back up with a huge box. When he opened it, one would have thought it was Fourth of July all over again. There were enough arsenals to blow up a city.

"Now that's what I'm talking about," Isaac said as he reached in and grabbed his holster. "Come back to Daddy, baby."

Keith started sweating. "Isaac, think about what you're doing."

Fastening the holster, Isaac ignored Keith. He rummaged through the box.

"We should go back to the hospital and join that prayer group. We need to be praying for Donavan, Nina and Mickey."

Isaac found what he was looking for. Cold eyes turned to Keith. Cold and dangerous. "Look man, this is who I am. Now, if Mickey is stupid enough to throw rocks at me, I'm not going to bow down and pray for him." His lip curled as he shoved his Glock in the holster. "I'm gon' kill him."

Grabbing another gun and strapping it to his right ankle

he told Keith, "You might want to run on back to the hospital. 'Cause this is where things get bloody."

Awake for almost an hour now, Nina could barely move. Her body ached, but nothing could surpass the ache in her heart. Tears stung her eyes as she tried to comprehend what had happened. She couldn't believe what the doctor told her. But the pain she felt at his cruel words was common to what she'd felt the day her first baby's life had been sucked out of her body.

*"You can lay here for a little while, dear. Don't worry about getting up until you feel better."*

*Nina wanted to ask the nurse how long does feeling better take? When do you get over killing someone you were supposed to protect?*

*Tears of regret and anger trickled down her face as she clutched her empty stomach. How had she allowed herself to be talked into aborting her baby?*

*She was no better than her mother. But, at least her mother brought her into this world before discarding her. Maybe she was worse than the woman who left her on the doorsteps of Children's Services and never looked back.*

*A scream escaped from the curtain-divided room Nina had just left. What's wrong with these people? Don't they take time to clean up the blood from the previous patient? Or do they just let it dry on their hands. She wanted to yank those curtains open, take that woman's legs off those stir-ups, and tell her to run. Get out before it's too late. Before they suck your baby out of you. And, and . . .*

*Her hand covered her mouth as sobs of regret escaped. What had her baby been? Should she have bought pink ribbons or blue shirts with sail boats on them? She'd never know. Life had been just that cruel.*

\* \* \*

A knock on her door jerked Nina from sorrows past. Wiping her eyes she turned and greeted Elizabeth.

"Hey. Dr. Hamilton said you wanted to see me."

Nina tried to smile at her friend. She really did. But too many cracks in the heart can break a smile. Crying was easier. So that's what she did.

Elizabeth rushed over to the bed and hugged her. "Ah, Nina. It's going to be all right."

Tightly holding Elizabeth's arm, Nina sobbed. "They won't let me see my son."

"You can't get up, Nina. You'll see Donavan soon enough."

Nina's face contorted. "Just tell me the truth. Is he dead?"

Elizabeth hugged her friend just a little tighter. Mindful of the surgery she'd just undergone, but mindful of the pain she was feeling. "He's hanging in there. He'll make it, Nina. You'll see."

"It's bad though, isn't it?"

Elizabeth stood up straight and looked her friend in the eye. "I'm not going to lie to you. You're right. Donavan was hurt pretty bad." She hung her head and let out a gust of hot air. "He's in a coma, Nina."

Wallowing from side to side, she felt the pain of each movement, but didn't care. "Oh, God. I can't lose him too. Not my son, Lord. Not *this* son."

Elizabeth stood by Nina's bed. She stroked her hair but said nothing. Sometimes words get lost in grief. Sometimes comfort comes not in the words said, but in being there.

"What am I going to do? What am I going to do?" Back and forth, Nina turned, asking the same question over and over again.

Humming, Elizabeth stroked her friend's hair. Tears rolled back and mingled with the sweat in Nina's hair. Nina kept asking the same question.

Finally, as an answer, Elizabeth sang: "Though the storms

keep on raging in my life, and sometimes it's hard to tell the night from day. Still this hope that lies within is reassured. If I keep my eyes upon the distant shore, I know He'll lead me safely to that special place He has prepared."

"What was God thinking, Elizabeth? How could this have happened to us?"

"And, if the storms don't cease. And if the winds keep on blowing in my life, my soul has been anchored in the Lord."

It had been a hard lesson, but Elizabeth had learned how to anchor her soul in the Lord. When things were going well, and even when everything went wrong, she would stand for Jesus. And now she would stand in the gap for her friend.

Nina calmed a little. Stopped rocking and listened. Elizabeth sang a couple more verses. Nina's eyes became heavy. She pulled the cover up to her chin and snuggled.

Charles appeared at the door with lilies in his hand. He had this I'm-so-into-you look on his face, as he gazed at his love. Elizabeth connected with him for the first time since meeting him. Felt his pain. She leaned over and whispered to Nina, "Charles is here. Do you want me to leave the two of you alone?"

Groggily, Nina told her, "No. Don't want to see Charles. The doctor said I can't have anymore children. Don't know how to tell Charles."

Charles heard Nina's declaration. The flowers in his hand fell to the floor. He turned and walked away from Nina's room.

# 24

Keith had a decision to make. He could strap up and follow his boy, or he could do what he knew was right. He hated snitches, but Isaac was about to destroy himself with some of that eye-for-an-eye, tooth-for-a-tooth stuff. He and Isaac had come too far to let it end on death row like this. Keith caught a cab back to the hospital, hoping that Charles was still there.

He was there all right; in the bathroom crying like somebody had beat him up on the play ground and stole his lunch money. "What's wrong," Keith asked when he saw the assistant DA in such a state.

Charles leaned against the bathroom wall. "My mama is going to be so disappointed. How am I going to explain this to her?"

Confusion was set on Keith's face. "Explain what? Man, what are you talking about?"

Charles pointed a daggered finger toward the door. "That animal destroyed my dreams. He took everything away from me."

"Nina is alive, man. What are you talking about?"

Charles bent over and dried his eyes with the back of his hand. "She can't have kids. The doctor confirmed it."

Dang. Keith wanted to cry himself. How could someone as sweet as Nina, as loving and kind hearted as she, be destroyed like this?

The bathroom door creaked open. Keith and Charles yelled, "Get out," in unison.

As the door closed back, Keith slid to the ground, crushing his hand to his mouth. If the truth was told, he had loved Nina for almost as long as Isaac had. Actually, he'd fallen in love with Nina when Isaac was still playing around, not knowing what was good for him. But, as far as Keith was concerned, Nina had always belonged to his best friend. That made her off limits to him. So, he'd put his feelings in check and tried to move on with life. That didn't stop him from hurting for her.

*Get yourself together.* He wiped his oceanous eyes and turned to Charles. "We've got to do something about Mickey. He's got to pay for what he's done."

Pacing the length of the bathroom, Charles roared, "I'd like to kill him."

"Unless I get your help, he will definitely be dead within the hour."

Charles turned to Keith. "What are you talking about?" He looked around, as if just noticing something. "Where's Isaac?"

Keith stood. "Look, I'm going to need your help. I think we can get Mickey, but I need you to take off your DA hat for a minute. Can you do that?"

"If it will help put this guy away, you name it. I'm there."

Shots fired on the West Side of Dayton was like a well-manicured lawn in the suburbs—constant. So when Isaac blasted three shots into the crack house door on Stewart Street before kicking it in, the news cameras did not start rolling.

"Where's he at," Isaac asked as he grabbed the first person unlucky enough to get close to him.

Crack fumes penetrated the air. The place smelled like sewage and waste. Looked like one of those houses the police busted into that had clothes and trash mixed together on the floor. Like clothes hangers and trash bags were a luxury trifflin' people couldn't afford. Isaac twisted his nose as he smelled first, then saw dog poop on the dirty floor.

"Who? Who you looking for?" a man with dreadlocks asked.

Isaac shoved his gun in the thick bushes of the man's locks. Men and women moved around them like zombies. Isaac ignored them. Glaring at his victim, he left no doubt what his intentions were. "Mickey, fool. Now start talking."

"Mickey left here about an hour ago. He's on Cincinnati Street, man. Come on, put the gun down."

Isaac backed out the door, gun still trained on Dreddy's head. "If you see him before I do, tell him to go kiss his kids goodnight."

Keith kept blowing up Isaac's cell phone as he drove toward his destination. Isaac started to turn the ringer off on Keith's third try, but thought better of it. What if something's gone wrong? What if Donavan or Nina got worse since he left the hospital? Reluctantly, he answered the phone. "What?"

"Where are you?"

"I'm on my way to meet Mickey. That punk wasn't on Lexington or Stewart, but he's in his house on Cincinnati Street. I'm sure of it."

"I'll meet you there," Keith told him.

Sarcastically, Isaac asked, "Is the prayer meeting over? You ready to do something other than fold your hands and bow your head?"

"Isaac, wait on me. There is a better way to handle this. Listen to what God is speaking to your heart."

Shaking his head, Isaac told his friend, "The devil wants me back in, Keith. I've got to play this one out."

"He hung up!" Slamming the phone against the dashboard, Keith yelled, "Dear God, don't let this happen."

"Hand me that phone," Charles told Keith.

With a look of skepticism on his face, Keith asked, "Who are you calling?"

"The police. Who do you think?"

Wildly, Keith shook his head. "Oh, no, uh-uh. You told me you would help Isaac, not put him back in prison."

"Look, can you stop that man from doing exactly what he pleases?"

Nobody could stop Isaac once his mind was made up. Keith didn't bother to share that bit of truth.

"Just what I thought. And I'm definitely not going to try to stop him; not with that gun in his hand." Charles reached out for the phone again. "Our best bet is to get the police over there and try to defuse the situation before *your* maniac kills *my* maniac."

# 25

Nina was jolted out of her sleep by a startling revelation. "Oh, my God!" she screamed.

Elizabeth jumped. She had been dozing in the seat next to Nina's bed. "W-what's wrong?"

Nina held onto the bed rails. "Did anybody call Isaac?"

Elizabeth sat back down and exhaled. "Girl, you had me scared for a moment. Yeah, Isaac was here. He spent the night in Donavan's room."

Nina laid there for a moment and calmed herself. She squeezed her friend's hand. "Thanks for being here with me."

"Where else would I be at a time like this?"

"Well, thanks anyway." Nina tried to smile at her friend, but her heart wasn't in it. "Did Kenneth come with you?"

"He wanted to, but one of us had to stay with the girls. You know I've got two teenagers on my hands now."

Laughing, Nina smacked Elizabeth's hand. "Leave my girls alone. They are perfect angels. How are Erin and Danae doing, anyway?"

"Erin is beside herself. You know she's going to be a senior in high school next term." Putting her feet in the chair,

Elizabeth sat Indian style. "Danae is still constantly studying and getting good grades. She gets that from Kenneth."

"Girl, they grow up too fast, don't they?"

"Tell me about it. The more I watch them grow, the more I wish I could have another . . ."

Nina turned her face toward the wall, away from her friend.

Elizabeth put her hand up to her mouth. "Nina, I'm so sorry. I-I didn't mean—"

Holding up her hand, Nina told Elizabeth, "Don't worry about it."

Silence kept them company as Nina continued to stare at the wall.

Breaking the silence, Elizabeth asked, "Can I get you anything?"

Nina turned back toward her friend and asked, "Can you ask Isaac to come in here? I want to know how Donavan is doing."

"Isaac's not here."

"I thought you said he was with Donavan."

"That was earlier."

Alarm bells were ringing throughout her system. With trepidation, Nina asked, "Where is Isaac, Elizabeth?"

"I'm not sure. Some guy came to see him this morning. I think he was a friend of Donavan's."

Prodding her friend to continue, Nina asked, "What happened when the guy left?"

"He didn't leave. His name is Mark Smith. He's still sitting in the waiting room with everybody else. He mumbled something about feeling responsible for Donavan and some boy named JC."

"What happened to JC?"

Elizabeth shook her head. Her eyes were downcast. "He got killed the same night you and Donavan were shot."

Nina knuckled down on the bedrails. "Good Lord. I knew

Donavan and JC were up to something." She turned back to Elizabeth. "Who's in the waiting room?"

"Pastor McKinley, my brother and his wife, Charles . . ." Snapping her fingers, Elizabeth told her, "That's right, Charles left with Keith."

"Charles left with *Keith*?"

"Yeah, first Keith left with Isaac, then Keith came back by himself. Then Charles left with Keith."

Nina was getting a headache. "When did Isaac leave?"

"I already told you; after he talked with Mark."

Tears rolled down Nina's face as she closed her eyes and listened to her gut tell her that something was very wrong. But this time, her woman's intuition wasn't telling on her son, but his father. "Elizabeth, will you pray with me?"

Released for battle, Davison charged forward. He had a legion of angels with him. He'd gone into battle with many of these angels before. They were good at what they did, but sorrow accompanied him as he drew his sword. Casualties would come from this battle. All the forces of hell had conspired to get Isaac back on Satan's side.

Davison wasn't having it. This was his charge. Isaac wasn't going to fall prey to the wicked one, even if he had to give his life to assure it.

Satan's hellions approached them in mid-descent. Davison had a feeling that they wouldn't get the cloud dust off their feet before the party got started. "Get ready. Here they come," Davison said to his comrades.

The thunder clapped and lightening raged as the battle ensued.

When the heavenly and hellish swords clashed, the earthly system was jolted. Slithers of lightening flashed through the sky. Blow after thunderous blow, Davison cut his way through the masses of demons. His single-minded purpose was to get to Isaac. "Keep praying, saints. Keep praying!"

# 26

Mickey was drunk when Isaac walked in on him. So drunk that slapping him upside the head with his Glock was useless. Isaac did it anyway.

The head trauma caused Mickey to vomit on the already nasty, dirty floor.

Good, Isaac thought. Some of the drunk probably oozed out of him when he threw up. Now he'll be able to feel this kick.

"Urrrgggh!" Mickey screamed as Isaac kicked him in the back.

Isaac then sent a heavy handed blow to Mickey's head.

"Ah, man, that hurt." Mickey's wobbly hand reached for his gun. Isaac ripped it out of his holster, and kicked him again.

Several kilos decorated the dilapidated dining room table. Back in the day, Isaac would have killed this low-life, took his stuff, and sold it himself. Hadn't he just crawled back into his past? He might as well take that stash and get his grind on. He sure wasn't going to have a church job to go back to after this, and a man's gotta eat.

"I-Isaac, man, I'm sorry," Mickey said with a pained expression on his face.

Reaching down, Isaac grabbed a fist full of Mickey's shirt and pulled him up. "You messed with the wrong one, boy."

Nervously, Mickey laughed. "You know how I am, man. I just get to trippin' sometimes."

*Trippin'?* Was he crazy?

The answer to that stupid question was a resounding aboleet, aboleet, that's a yes, folks.

Although crazy, Mickey was no punk. He wasn't going out like a sucka, even if he was up against the great Isaac Walker. They tussled. Isaac dropped his gun. Mickey used that opportunity to swing.

With the way Isaac's jaw shook, Mickey could have been a contender. "What you think about that?" Mickey asked while shuffling his feet like a boxer. "Yeah, I ain't no easy win, nigga." He swung on Isaac again and connected.

Isaac grabbed him by the throat and drove him against the wall.

Mickey's breath whooshed from his body.

The wall buckled as Isaac slammed Mickey's head into it again and again. When he released him to grab his Glock, Mickey crumpled to the floor holding his throat. "Man, you're supposed to be a preacher."

Isaac smiled sinisterly. "That's why you're getting a two-for-one special today. A man who can kill you *and* eulogize your miserable funeral."

Isaac kicked Mickey in the face, then picked his gun off the floor and lifted it to Mickey's head. "What do you want on your tombstone, Mickey?"

Blood dripped from his mouth, but that didn't stop him from running it. "You tired of looking at yourself, Isaac? Is that why you want me dead?"

"You're nothing like me."

Mickey crawled on the floor like the animal he was. His

gold teeth weren't as sparkly with blood splattered on them. "I am what you made me. You taught me everything I know." Mickey's gun was in sight, he kept crawling toward it.

*Shoot him. No need for conversation. What are you waiting on? Don't you dare think about God. Just leave the Almighty-oh-so-busy-One out of this.* All these thoughts ran through Isaac's mind as Mickey reminded him of the man he used to be.

"I didn't teach you to kill kids."

Mickey's laughter bounced off the walls. He picked up his gun and fired. The bullet missed Isaac by a mile. Mickey stood, more confident now. "That bad little nigga needs to die."

Mickey tried to shoot at Isaac again but his clip was empty. Isaac squeezed the trigger of his gun—he had bullets and didn't miss. The only problem was that when Mickey stood up, Isaac had not re-aimed the gun. So, the bullet went into Mickey's left thigh.

"Urrrgggh!" Mickey dropped his gun and started jumping around while screaming. "You shot me! You shot me!"

The second bullet missed Mickey by half and inch. Slumping back to the ground, Mickey giggled through the pain. "Give me your phone, Isaac. I'm calling your pastor."

Isaac's cold eyes bore into him. "Right now, I suggest you call on Jesus."

"Forget Him. I'd rather call on the devil. He's the only one that's ever helped me," he told Isaac as he broke into his crazy man chant. "Oh, Satan, come help me. Oh, Satan, Isaac keeps shooting at your son. Oh, Satan; oh, my daddy, come help me now."

Isaac's hand shook. Mickey had no idea what he was asking for, but Isaac did. The devil would help him all right. He'd help him all the way to hell.

"I'm bleeding. Woo hoo!" His head flopped back and forth. "I'm a bloody mess. Losing con-scious . . . . ness." His words were slow and slurred.

Conflicted, Isaac pondered, should he pray or should he shoot? Finishing Mickey off would do the world a great service, but Mickey would bust hell wide open. Even this psychopath wasn't ready for the torment he'd suffer in hell. Isaac had already sent too many people there. Could he live with one more?

*What am I doing here? How could I have sunk so low again?* Isaac put his hand to his head, the one that didn't hold his Glock, and rubbed his temple. "Oh, God, I don't want to send him to hell. Help me!"

The door to the crack house opened and Keith and Charles rushed in. Isaac turned his gun on them, then lowered it.

Mickey pointed at Charles. "Thank you, Satan. I knew you'd rescue me."

# 27

Standing over his son's hospital bed, Isaac breathed a sigh of relief. The rage that boiled in him, at times, scared even him. He had escalated from verbal threats, to beat downs in the house of God. And finally, he had been in a crack house with a pistol in his hand, contemplating killing someone and stealing his dope.

He looked down at the comatose form of his son. Donavan had managed to get himself into more drama than an eleven . . . no, twelve-year-old should know. That's right, today was his son's birthday. Would he live to celebrate?

"Happy birthday, Donavan," Isaac said as he bent down and kissed his son on the forehead.

How could he blame his son for getting into all this mess? "You're just like your old man, Donavan. And that's nothing to be proud of, son."

Isaac would be in jail right now, if it wasn't for Charles. Or maybe his angel had finally shown up on the scene. Isaac shook his head. As much as he despised Charles for wanting to marry Nina, he also admired the way he stood up for him at the police station. He told the chief of police that since they were so inapt at finding Mickey, Isaac had to make a citizen's arrest. Charles also told the chief that Mickey had been shot in self-defense. Since Isaac had just as many cuts and bruises on his face as Mickey; coupled with the fact that Mickey also had gun powder residue on his hands, self-defense wasn't a hard case to prove.

When all was said and done, the police and the district attorney's office were so glad to finally have Mickey behind bars, they decided that one bullet wound to the leg was a whole lot less than Mickey had left his victims with.

"Don't leave town, Isaac. We might need to discuss this matter with you later," was all they said to him. Isaac didn't mind staying in town. His family was here.

He bowed his head low. "Thank you, Lord." He wasn't mad at God anymore, just at himself. At the situations in life that caused grown men to watch their sons repeat the same mistakes they'd made. Weary, Isaac sat down. His Bible was next to his son's bed, but he couldn't make himself pick it up. Instead, he decided to walk down the hall to Nina's room.

He didn't hate Charles Douglas III, but a strong dislike for the man rose up again as he saw him sitting in Nina's room. He wanted to turn and walk away. They were holding each other. Isaac could barely stand to watch, but they were crying.

Charles was saying, "I love you, Nina. You know I do."

Isaac could see Nina's face. She didn't look so sure. "Don't worry about it, Charles. I'll be all right."

"But I feel so bad. I just wish none of this had happened."

Nina pulled herself away from Charles. She carefully took off her engagement ring and handed it to him. "It wasn't your fault. As you've already told me, this happened to us because of something Donavan was involved in."

She wiped her eyes with her left arm since the other one was in a sling. "Could you hand me some tissue please?"

Charles grabbed a handful of tissue and handed them to Nina. She blew her nose the best she could with the use of one hand. "Thank you," she said, while wiping her nose.

Isaac felt like a peeping Tom, but he kept listening anyway.

Charles was shaking his head. "I don't know, Nina. I just wish things were different."

There was a cold look in Nina's eyes as she glared at Charles. "But they aren't. Don't worry about us. We'll be fine."

Charles got up and walked toward Isaac. He didn't look up though, almost as if he was ashamed to look Isaac in the eye.

Waving to Nina, Isaac approached her. She turned her face from his inspection and wiped away a few more tears.

"What's going on?" He tried to sound light hearted, but he wanted to know what Charles had said to put those tears in her eyes.

"Oh, nothing much," Nina said sarcastically. "I've just been shot, my son's in a coma, his father tried to kill the man who shot us, and my engagement has just been called off. But other than that, I live a drama-free life."

Isaac smiled wearily. "Okay, the first three I already knew about. What happened with your engagement?"

Tears sprang up again. She couldn't stop them if she wanted to. Isaac handed her some more tissue. She blotted her eyes. "Do me a favor, Isaac."

He stood over her. "Anything, Nina. Just tell me what you need."

"Would you go to JC's funeral? Somebody needs to be there to encourage his family."

Violently shaking his head, Isaac told her, "Ask anything else, Nina. I'll do it for you. Anything but that."

Tears cascaded down Nina's cheeks as she told him, "We've got to get past this, Isaac."

Isaac's hand lifted and he pointed in the direction of Donavan's room. "My son's in a coma, Nina. JC helped put him there. How can I get past that?"

Nina opened her mouth to respond, but Isaac held up his hand. "I don't want to discuss this anymore." He ran his hands through his hair to calm himself. "Anyway, you're just trying to change the subject. I want to know what happened to your engagement."

"I guess I forgot to mention one other thing. Dr. Hamilton says that children are out for me. Says my uterus was damaged beyond repair."

A mist covered Isaac's eyes as he plunked down in the chair Charles had vacated. "Ah, baby, I'm sorry." Old Charles must have been relieved to know that Mickey didn't come after Nina because of him. Gave him his walking papers, but he wouldn't say that to Nina.

"Do you remember when I told you about the abortion I had when I was seventeen?"

"Yeah. What about it?"

The tears wouldn't stop. "I've been having a hard time finishing my third book. It deals with a woman receiving forgiveness from God after having an abortion." Patting her eyes with the tissue, she continued. "I guess I still don't believe that God has forgiven me for what I did."

"Nina, the Lord loves you. You are sold out for Christ." Isaac wished to God that he could have been half as committed to the Lord as this woman. He would have to live with his demons, but not Nina. He continued encouraging her, "Why wouldn't God take your sin and cast it into the sea and choose not to remember it, just as His Word promises every believer?"

"I don't know," she answered him pitifully. "But when that doctor told me I wouldn't be able to have children, I felt like God had finally passed judgment against me."

"Well, you're wrong, Nina. This thing that happened to

you is awful. It makes me angry enough to want to hurt Mickey all over again, but it's not God's judgment against you. God sees you through the blood of Jesus, and you've been found innocent."

Patting the tissue against her eyes, she said, "Charles sure doesn't see me through the blood of Jesus. He sees me as broken."

"Charles's actions have nothing to do with God."

She touched Isaac's hand. "Thanks. I know you're right. I'm just glad that I found out now, that having children was more important to Charles than having me." Her tears burst forth again. "It just hurts, you know."

Isaac wanted to tell her that Charles wasn't worth her tears. The man obviously didn't trust God. Had no faith, or he would understand that God could change a doctor's report. But he had just shot a man because he didn't trust God to be all He could be in the situation. Too early to throw salt on another man's game.

# 28

Bishop Sumler marched around his office waiting for Cassandra to show up. He was fuming mad. Word had gotten back to him that Isaac had almost been arrested for trying to kill some worthless scum. He rolled his eyes heavenward. "Too many fires to put out, Lord Jesus."

Picking up the phone, he called Keith for the third time that day. He'd been calling Isaac too, but neither had bothered to answer their phones as of yet.

"Keith, call me. I need to know what's going on down there," Bishop yelled into the phone when the voicemail picked up. "These boys think they can solve their own problems," he huffed. "I make my living solving problems."

Knock. Knock.

"Come on in. What are you waiting for?"

Nervously, Cassandra stepped into Bishop's office. "You wanted to see me, sir?"

He pointed at the chair in front of his desk. "Sit down." He stood in front of her with his backside on the edge of his desk. "I want to know what happened. Why hasn't Isaac tried to call you since he's been gone?"

"Sir, I'm sure Isaac has a lot going on. He's probably too busy to think about me right now."

"Cut the bull, Cassandra. Isaac's in pain right now. His son's been shot. If anything, he's in need of some comfort. Why isn't he seeking you for it?"

She turned her face from Bishop's inspection. "Something happened between me and Isaac the night his son got shot."

"That's more like it." Bishop walked to his chair and sat behind his desk. "So, tell me. Why are you the last thing on Isaac's mind?"

Without looking up she replied, "I didn't want to say anything, but he tried to have sex with me when he came back from West Virginia, sir. I told him that I wasn't interested." She hunched her shoulders. "I guess he just wants a woman who'll put out."

Bishop leaned back in his seat and studied Cassandra. His laughter caused her head to raise. He stopped laughing and told her, "Now Cassandra, honey, you are my goddaughter and I love you. But I wasn't born yesterday. I brought you here 'cause I knew you would put out. Only trouble is, Isaac is not interested in that right now. I thought you would be smart enough to see that."

He stood and paced the room. "That boy wants to do things right for God. Don't you see how the congregation goes crazy when he preaches? The boy is anointed. I brought you here to be his wife. I have a church I want him to take over. With your voice and his preaching, there would be no end to how much Isaac could earn for the ministry."

Embarrassed by the lie Bishop caught her in, Cassandra lowered her head and said, "I don't know what you want me to do. I blew it with Isaac already."

"You just let me worry about that." He stood at his window and gazed out. In his mind's eye he could see the greatness that God put in Isaac. The boy was going to be somebody one day. Maybe even bigger than T.D. Jakes, and he was going to ride all the way to fame and fortune with him; kind of like Mike Tyson and Don King, but in a spiritual sense.

"He's in love with his baby's mama," Bishop said, as if he wasn't talking to the woman he wanted Isaac to marry. "Thank God she's engaged to someone else. The woman is not ministry material. She can't draw a crowd like you can with that voice of yours." He'd taken care of the Nina problem once before when he sent Denise to her house and had her lie about being pregnant by Isaac. That didn't work, so now he was just praying for this marriage of hers to come quickly.

Turning back to Cassandra, he said, "You are ministry material. You just need to learn how to keep your dress down until somebody asks you for what you got."

"JC's funeral is today. It's going to be at Wheat Funeral Home, at one o'clock."

Isaac knew Nina wanted him to care, wanted him to do something. But as God was his witness, he couldn't find a caring bone within him. Not for JC. "Why would that information interest me?"

Elizabeth had gone home that morning. The waiting room had emptied out. This was Donavan's third day in a coma. Isaac had talked Dr. Hamilton into moving Nina and Donavan into the same room. The doctor agreed that since Nina couldn't get up, she would probably feel better being in closer proximity to her son. So Isaac's bed was a chair and a stool. He positioned them between Donavan's and Nina's beds. They had been talking like this since Elizabeth left, but he hadn't expected Nina to bring up the funeral again.

"Just thought you might want to know. I thought you might want to go over there and support the family."

"Guess you thought wrong. I'm not going to that boy's funeral. I don't care how his family is doing." He lifted his hand to stop her from saying anything else. "Look, Nina, I've got a lot of demons I'm trying to deal with right now. I don't need to add anything else to my list. Okay?"

Nina tried to lift up so she could look Isaac in the eyes. The pain was unbearable. "Don't you think your father has a lot to do with those demons you're dealing with?"

"Let it go, okay?"

"I'm not going to let it go. You have to get over this hatred you carry around."

He jumped out of his chair. "Stop judging me. I've got enough to deal with."

She closed her eyes and flopped her head against her pillow. "Isaac, let God deal with your problems. He can forgive you for what you've done, but you need to forgive too."

"Well, hello pot."

Nina's eyes flew open. "What's that supposed to mean?"

"You know what I'm talking about. You've got the nerve to lecture me. I'm not the only one that needs to accept God's forgiveness and move on. You've been holding yourself and God hostage for something you did as a teenager." He stalked out of the room throwing back, "Don't you think it's time for you to let go?"

If he had waited for Nina's response, Isaac would have seen the tears as they flowed down her face. He would have known that she had leaned into God's forgiving arms and said, "I'm sorry, please forgive me. Help me to accept your forgiveness." But he hadn't waited. He'd stormed out of the room like a mad dog.

## 29

He left the hospital with his mind set on showing Nina that he could put things behind him. He could let stuff go. JC's funeral was scheduled for one o'clock. If he did fifty miles per hour up Salem, he'd make it to Wheat Funeral Home at about ten or fifteen after. Nina was too goodie-goodie. Always more concerned about others than herself. JC's trifflin' mama and daddy didn't need no prayer. They needed a butt whupping.

Isaac parked his car in the funeral home parking lot at about seven minutes after one. He got out of his car, took a deep breath and walked toward the entrance. Before he could get inside the funeral home, he passed by a couple of disgruntled family members. They were mad about having to chip in their last twenty dollars to bury JC when he still owed one of them fifty dollars.

Isaac shook his head. "Too trifflin' to get an insurance policy for their son," he mumbled as he opened the door and stepped into the lobby area of the funeral home. Thugs and gold-diggers littered the lobby. They were laughing and high-fiving one another, talking about the last funeral they'd attended and how they went to the graveyard and toasted their boy with some Cognac.

Two ushers timidly entered the lobby with their index finger to their lips. "Shhhhh."

"My fault, man," one of the gold teethed thugs told them.

"The service has started. Can you please take your seats?" the usher said.

One by one, they all filed in like a cop had just picked them up for outstanding warrants and they were lining up for mug shots and fingerprints.

A teenage girl was singing, "Going Up Yonder" when Isaac took his seat in the back. The smirk on his face said that he didn't believe that JC was going up yonder. Why didn't they just tell the truth? Somebody needs to come up with a song that says something like, *I ain't right, I ain't never been right. I died like a fool and now I'm in hell.* But they probably wanted rhymes and rhythm, rather than reality.

Cell phones were going off two at a time. Black folks were leaning over in their seats or stepping out to answer their phones like they were some kind of tycoons making billion dollar deals that just couldn't wait until the end of a pesky funeral.

Isaac spotted Lou in the seventh row from the front. Lou waved and Isaac nodded in return. Mickey would have most likely sat next to him if he wasn't on lock-down right now. That's how Mickey and his crew got down. They'd kill someone, go to their funeral to watch their family mourn, then they'd go to the cemetery and spit on their grave. In the end, a bullet and disrespect was all a hustler had coming.

The song ended and Pastor Paul O. Mitchell took his place behind the podium. His hair was freshly trimmed. His black double-breasted suit emphasized the grief stricken expression on his face. Putting his Bible on the podium, he lowered his head. The congregation watched, Isaac watched, but still, he said nothing.

Shaking himself, Pastor Paul looked toward the people and said, "I am so tired of this."

Isaac was struck by the sincerity of the man before him. He knew of Pastor Paul, had heard of the ever growing Revival Center Ministries on James H. McGee Boulevard. He had heard about the revelations that God gave this young pastor. He'd even heard about Pastor Paul's dynamic preaching style. But he'd never heard a word about Pastor Paul coming from the streets. Pastor Paul had not been a hustler like he had—but his sorrow showed that he cared nonetheless.

"I don't want to do another funeral like this," Pastor Paul continued. "I don't want to lose another young man to the streets." He moved from behind the podium and addressed the congregation. "How many of you out there are drug dealers?"

Isaac smirked. Like they are just going to wave their hands and say, "Here I am, Mr. Policeman, come and get me." The smirk left Isaac's face when numerous hands went up.

"How many of you are prostitutes or drug addicts?" Again, hands flew up all over the building. "Now how many of you want to be free?" Pastor Paul screamed the word *free*, and the place exploded with praise to God as one person after the next stood. Pastor Paul unbuttoned his jacket and threw it off. "All your life people have told you that you weren't going to be anything. You wouldn't be able to get out of the hell you're living in. But I came to tell you today . . . that devil lied!"

Isaac's mouth hung open. Never had he heard a man preach with such authority and power. Did Pastor Paul truly believe that these people could change? Isaac had to ask himself why he didn't believe it. Why had he turned away from these people instead of reaching out and showing them the right way?

"Mike, come over here," Pastor Paul called out to a young man seated on the platform with him. As Mike walked toward him, Pastor Paul told the congregation, "This young man is one of my armor bearers. But before Jesus changed Mike's life, he was doing so much crazy stuff in the streets that he tattooed the word 'Thug' on his arm." Pastor Paul handed the microphone to Mike and told him, "Tell them a little bit about yourself."

With his head held low, Mike took the microphone. He shook his head as he stood there for a moment. Lifting the mic to his mouth he told the people, "I was snorting about five grams of cocaine a day. Smoking, drinking, sexing up a lot of women—doing all kinda nasty stuff, but God saved me anyhow." He lifted his head as a holy boldness rose in him. "Now I just want to be right. I found out that if God is for me, He is more than the whole world against me." With that, Mike handed the microphone back to Pastor Paul and took his seat.

"My God can change lives," Pastor Paul shouted. "Isaiah 59 says, *Behold, the Lord's hand is not shortened that it cannot save, neither his ears heavy that he cannot hear—but your iniquities have separated you from your God.*

"But don't give up hope my people. Because another verse in the Bible goes on to say, *All day long I have stretched forth my hand to a gainsaying and disobedient people.* If you know that God has been stretching out His hand to you while you have been disobeying His laws, I want you to stand."

Isaac looked around. Along with numerous hustlers, JC's mother and father were standing. He looked toward the back of the room and surprise gripped him as he not only saw Eloise, Mickey's mother—but he saw her stand up and raise her hands to God.

"If you really want deliverance, all you've got to do is

stretch yourself toward God. Remember, His hand is not too short to save. I'm going to pray for you all and then I'm going to get back to the business of eulogizing JC."

By the time Pastor Paul finished his message, Isaac was ready to let JC rest in peace.

## 30

Back at the hospital, Isaac went into Nina and Donavan's room, burdened down by the fact that he had gone against God's will when he attacked Mickey. Pastor Paul had opened his eyes to real ministry; helping to bring others up, rather than leaving them behind. He'd received that revelation at JC's funeral. He just didn't know what he was going to do with it. Walking over to Nina's bed, he checked to make sure she was really asleep. Then he lifted his Bible from Donavan's nightstand and turned to Psalm 119.

Isaac felt like a fraud, like one of those jack-legged preachers that Nina often spoke of. How could he sit down and open this Bible after what he had done? Bottom line, he had failed God. That knowledge wore heavily on him.

But how was it that he still felt God's call on his life? Why would God want him? Plagued by questions that received no answers, he read God's precious Word.

*How can a young man cleanse his ways?*
*By taking heed according to Your Word.*

*With my whole heart I have sought You; Oh, let me
not wander from Your commandments!*

As Isaac continued reading the Word of God, the breath of
life was being blown back into him. This particular Psalm
had 173 verses, but Isaac didn't care. He kept reading:

*I long for Your salvation, O Lord, and Your law is my
delight.
Let my soul live, and it shall praise You; and let Your
judgments help me.
I have gone astray like a lost sheep; seek Your
servant, for I do not forget Your commandments.*

He bowed to the Lord and prayed. "Against you only,
Lord, have I sinned and done this wicked thing. Create in me
a clean heart and renew a right spirit within me. Let my soul
live, Lord, and I will give you praise."

His gaze swept the room and found his son. "Lord, I know
I have no right to ask. You've already shown me more mercy
than I deserve, but please, Lord, allow my son to live."

He stayed on the floor for another hour, praying and peti-
tioning God. "Lord, I'll never stray from your will again.
Thank you for forgiving me." He rebuked the demonic forces
that were trying to place strongholds over his life and his
son's. He rebuked 'til his rebuker was worn out, and God
was listening. Isaac was sure of it.

Isaac lifted his eyes and saw tears flowing down Nina's
beautiful face as she silently prayed. Maybe she was praying
for him. Thank you, Jesus.

Donavan's right arm jerked. He squinted once, then twice.
Isaac ran to get the nurse. "Look, something's happened," he
told the nurse, as he explained what he'd witnessed.

After standing over Donavan for two minutes without seeing any movement, the nurse told him, in a very calm voice, "It might have just been reflex motions. Come and get me if something else occurs." She walked out.

Isaac smiled over at Nina. "It wasn't just reflex. He's waking up."

Nina looked heavenward. "I sure hope so." She picked up her Bible.

This was Donavan's fourth day under. Isaac and Nina spent the night praying, pleading, and crying.

Massaging his son's arm, Isaac spoke his heart. "I can't wait 'til you wake up. I want to show you how important you are to me."

Isaac sat and watched Nina read her Word. She was the sun, moon and the stars to him. Everything that is beautiful. If only she knew it. "What are you reading?" he asked her.

She looked up and gave him a half-hearted smile. "I'm searching the scriptures for verses on forgiveness. This has been harder for me than I could have imagined."

Isaac nodded. "Hard on us all."

Nina's head fell backward, her lip twisted downward. "I'm working on forgiving myself. I think that will help me to forgive the person who shot us. It's hard, you know. I mean, even knowing that my baby is in heaven, I still live with the guilt of being the one that sent him there."

Isaac could relate. He had sent a lot of brothers in the opposite direction. Guilt like that didn't go away overnight.

Isaac stared deep into Nina's hazel eyes and asked, "What about me, Nina? Can you forget about some of the mistakes I've made, and trust *me*?"

Nina was silent. Trust was a big word. Too many issues between them. She wanted to respond, give him a glimmer of hope. But the words wouldn't come. Thankfully, Keith strutted into the room at that awkward moment.

"Hey, black people," he called out to them.

Nina smiled at her friend. Her rescuer, whether he knew it

or not. "It's about time you showed your ugly face around here."

Keith rubbed the well-groomed mustache on his honey-coated face. "Woman, you know I am far from ugly. Now, if you had been talking about this guy," he pointed at Isaac, "I could understand. Women hate to look at him."

"I know," Nina said, laughing. "I suffer every time he comes over."

"Okay, okay, enough jokes on me. How'd you even get back here? This is a restricted area," Isaac told Keith as he pointed towards the door. "Go back out there and wait until we get bored enough to be bothered with you."

"Man, I got tired of waiting. I told that nurse that I had to get back to Chicago. Bishop Sumler's blowing up my cell phone. He says that one of us has got to see this building project through. But I wanted to see my godson before I left."

"Unnnn."

Isaac, Keith and Nina each heard the unintelligible sound. But comprehension did not set in until the next, "Unnnn."

"Oh, my God!" Isaac leaped to Donavan's side. His eyes were open.

"He's trying to say Uncle Keith," Keith said proudly.

"No, he's not," Isaac said while rolling his eyes, irritation clearly in his voice.

"Yes, he is." Keith walked over to the bed and smiled down at Donavan. "Boy, if I'd have known that you were waiting to hear my voice, I would have busted through security sooner."

"That loud mouth of yours probably disturbed his sleep," Isaac said in a disgruntled manner. Truthfully, he didn't care what did it. His son was awake. Let the rejoicing begin. "Thank you, Lord!"

\* \* \*

Three days later, after having numerous tests run on both Nina and Donavan, and finding them to be in good health; they were thrown out of the hospital. Isaac moved into Nina's guest room, which doubled as a sewing room. "I'm staying, and that's that," he told Nina, when she tried to protest.

A nurse came to the house once daily to bathe Nina. For the next week, she was bedridden. Donavan needed little help. Once he woke up, he was in rare form. Isaac made him rest a few hours each day, but for the most part, Donavan was feeling very little pain. It seemed that God had him in a deep sleep to totally heal his body. When her week of confinement was over, Isaac fluffed a couple of pillows on the living room couch and sat Nina down with some magazines and the book *Jezebel* by Jacquelin Thomas, one of Nina's favorite authors.

Nina tried to settle in, but Isaac and Donavan were in the kitchen. She could hear them arguing over something Isaac had fixed.

"I'm not going to eat that," Donavan told him.

"Boy, you better eat everything on your plate. Don't nobody have food for you to waste."

"Mama," Donavan yelled as he ran out of the kitchen. Actually, he walked kind of fast; healed though he was, running was out of the question for awhile. "Look at this, Mama." He dangled a dark piece of toast in Nina's face. "It's burnt and Daddy says I've gotta eat it."

Isaac walked out of the kitchen laughing. "I guess you've never heard of a burnt offering. Boy, go bless that food and eat it."

Donavan stomped back into the kitchen while Isaac handed Nina her breakfast. Nina grabbed Isaac's arm and asked him to sit for a moment. "Can I ask you something?"

"What's up?"

"What you're doing for me and Donavan is wonderful, but don't you think you need to go find your father?"

Here we go again. "Look, Nina. I'm grateful for what you're trying to do, but you've got to give me some space on that one."

"All I'm saying is—"

Isaac held up his hands. "I tried, Nina. Okay?" He stood up and paced the room. He didn't want to tell her about the time he went to Usually Wrong's house. That would just be another strike against him. Running his hands through his hair, he looked back at Nina. "Do you remember that movie, *Antwone Fisher*?"

Nina nodded. "It was a good movie."

"Yeah, well I could only watch it once, because it really got to me. The part that hit home for me was when he was in Denzel's office, talking about how he felt as a kid." Isaac walked over to the window and looked out. "Antwone Fisher said something about rainy days, and that for one kid it rained too much." He turned back to face Nina and sat on the window ledge. "That's how I feel when I think about my childhood. The rain never stopped. And every time I try to go back, I just get drenched all over again."

Isaac looked like a little lost boy. Nina wanted to take him in her arms and rescue him from the rain, from the pain, and the unfairness of it all, but that was God's job. At that moment, it was as if God had opened her eyes so that she could see Isaac. Not for who he was today, or yesterday. She saw the man he would become. It impressed her; made her look a little deeper. It caused her to speak of things only God could have imparted.

"Isaac, there is a latter rain that will fall on you. It will wipe away all the pain that life has brought to you. Trust God, Isaac. Your latter will be greater than anything you've ever known." She'd recently told their son about his latter days being greater than his beginning. She believed with all her heart that father and son would grow in God and handle the mantle placed on them with grace.

"If only God could be that merciful," Isaac said with sorrow etched on his face.

Nina stared at the man seated before her, trying to understand his complexities. *Who is he, Lord? What is he destined to be?*

**Great in my eyes,** she heard the Lord whisper into her spirit.

Isaac stood, pointed at her ham, eggs and toast. "I hope yours isn't too burnt. I've never been much of a cook."

Subject changed. "Well, when I get off this couch, I'll have to teach you a few tricks."

He devoured her with his eyes. "I'd like that."

They allowed themselves to get stuck in time for a moment; back to a time when they mattered to one another.

But it was so long ago, and so many things had happened to them since, Nina couldn't allow herself to linger. She turned her head and examined the eggs. "I'm sure this will be just fine. Thank you, Isaac."

He sat next to her and adjusted her pillow. "That's what I'm here for. Do you need anything else?"

She wouldn't meet his gaze. Couldn't look up. He might be smiling, and she'd have to see those dimples that used to drive her wild. "I'm fine." She waved him away. "Just go see about your son, and stop fussing over me." *Please!*

# 31

The break Bishop Sumler was waiting for came on a Tuesday. Marvin Walker came into his church looking for his son. Bishop Sumler didn't even know Isaac had a daddy. So much for total disclosure.

"Can someone tell me how I can get in touch with Isaac Walker," he asked Bishop Sumler's secretary just as the preacher happened by.

Once Bishop found out who the man was, he took him in his office and called Keith to get Nina's address. When he hung up, he looked over at Marvin. "Are you aware of the recent tragedy involving Isaac's son?"

Marvin leaned forward. "No. I just came here to see if I could talk to Isaac." He shrugged. "Make amends for past wrongs. But please tell me, what happened to my grandson?"

"Your grandson and his mother were shot a couple of weeks ago. A drive-by incident." Bishop wrote the Dayton address on a piece of paper and handed it to Marvin. "Isaac has been staying in Dayton to take care of them."

"Good Lord, I had no idea," Marvin said as he closed his eyes and ran his hand through his hair.

"Let me ask you something, Mr. Walker. How is your relationship with Isaac right now?"

Marvin shook his head and frowned. "It's nonexistent. To tell you the truth, I have only spoken to my son once in twenty years. He doesn't want anything to do with me."

"Really? Well, do you think it's a good idea to travel to Dayton to see someone who doesn't want to see you?"

"It's a horrible idea," Marvin admitted. "But if my grandson's been hurt, I've got to go. I've missed out on so much with my son, he may never want to have anything to do with me. But maybe I can make it up with my grandson." Hope grew in Marvin's eyes as he thought of a possible second chance.

Just what Sumler wanted to hear. "I think I might know how to reunite the two of you." He smiled at Marvin and picked up the phone again.

Within minutes, Cassandra was walking through Bishop's door. Her long jean skirt swept the floor. "You wanted to see me, sir?"

Bishop Sumler stood to greet Cassandra. "Yes, dear. I wanted to introduce you to someone."

She turned in Marvin's direction.

"This is Isaac's father."

Cassandra gasped. "You're kidding," she said gleefully.

Marvin stood. "I'm afraid he's not. Whether Isaac wants me to be or not, I'm his father."

She shook hands with the man she fully intended to make her father-in-law. "Well it's nice to meet you."

"Mr. Walker will be traveling to Dayton to see Isaac and his grandson. I thought that you might like to accompany him." Turning to Marvin, Bishop Sumler said, "Cassandra and Isaac are practically engaged. If anybody can convince Isaac to speak with you, she can."

# 32

Just barely seven o'clock in the morning and someone was already banging on the door. Isaac walked to the door in a pair of boxers and his thick black bathrobe. He opened the door, and just as unwanted as ever, Charles blew into his world.

He gave Isaac's attire more than a brief glance and asked, "Where are Nina and Donavan?"

"Sleep, where I'd like to be."

Rolling his eyes, Charles said, "Can you wake them? This is important."

Isaac walked off without answering Charles. He knocked on Nina's door and told her that the *assistant* DA wanted to talk with them. He then went down the hall and barged in Donavan's room unannounced. He'd already decided that the Privacy Act didn't include his son. He was going to stick his nose in everything that concerned him, including entering a room unannounced. "Get up, boy. We've got company."

Rolling over, Donavan asked, "Who's here this early in the morning?"

"The DA," Isaac told him. He left off *assistant* while talking to his son. But for some reason, he needed Nina to understand that Charles Douglas III wasn't running the show. Petty, he knew; but, hey, whatever works.

Donavan frowned. "What's he doing here?"

"You just get dressed and bring yourself downstairs." Isaac picked up a sweatshirt off Donavan's floor and threw it at him. "Now."

"Good morning, Charles," Nina said as the four of them sat in her living room.

"How've you been?" Charles asked.

"I'm making it. What can we do for you," she asked, keeping it real business-like.

Isaac eyed her, trying to see if any of that I-want-you-back-oo-baby stuff was behind that business-like tone.

"I thought you might like to know that we're going for the death penalty," Charles told Nina with a satisfied glint in his eyes.

Heartbreaking. Nina bent her head. Tears wouldn't come for Mickey, but that didn't stop her heart from aching.

Fury blazed through Charles's eyes. "What's wrong with you, Nina? Don't you dare pray for that animal."

"I feel sorry for him, Charles. I can't help that," Nina replied, lifting her head.

"Even after everything he's done to us—I mean, to you and Donavan?" Outrage was written across Charles's face.

Holding Charles's gaze, she told him, "I have chosen to forgive him. Some days my choice is easy, some days it's a burden."

Isaac couldn't help but admire Nina's ability to forgive, even after all Mickey had done to her. It was tough to admit, but he was in Charles's corner on this one. Burn Mickey, burn.

"What do you need from us?" Donavan asked.

Charles calmed himself. He managed to project pure professionalism as he said, "As you know, you and your mom are about the only two victims this animal . . . Mickey has left alive. We need both of you to testify. But it is your testimony," he looked directly at Donavan, "that will get us a conviction."

"Why me?" Donavan asked nervously.

"You are the only one that can connect Mickey with JC. We need your testimony, Donavan. Can you do it?"

Tears glistened in Donavan's eyes. He looked from his mother to his father. "Are you guys ashamed of me?"

Nina reached out to hug her wayward son. "Never."

"No matter what you've done, we'll never be ashamed or turn our backs on you," Isaac chimed in.

Donavan wiped his eyes and looked at his father. "Sometimes, I'm ashamed of myself. I feel like I've let you and Mom down."

Isaac looked to Charles. "What about immunity?"

"If Donavan testifies, nothing he says will be held against him. I promise you that."

Sitting next to Donavan, Isaac said, "I'll tell you what, son. Mickey has hurt a lot of families. So, when you get on the stand and tell what you know, I will be very proud of you indeed."

Half smiling, Donavan turned to Charles and told him. "You've got yourself a stoolie, Mr. Douglas."

They took a few more minutes to discuss the case, then Nina got up and slowly walked Charles to the door. They huddled a little too close at the front door for Isaac's comfort. He would have given anything to know what Charles whispered in her ear. Why was she still standing there talking to him? She must like getting played.

He wasn't going to sit there and watch this pathetic scene. He got up and stormed out of the living room. "Come on, Donavan. Let me fix you some breakfast."

"Nooo," Donavan screamed. "Mama said she was going to fix the breakfast this morning."

Donavan sat on the stool next to the stove and watched his father scorch some bacon and drown a few eggs in a skillet full of grease. Gulping, he wondered how clogged his arteries could get before they ceased to function.

The thought of death by grease sent his mind on a journey. Back to the hospital. Back to his coma. "Dad, can I tell you something?"

Isaac flipped a couple of strips of bacon. "Shoot."

Donavan pointed at the skillet. "For the love of God, man, take the bacon out already. How burnt do you want it?"

"Shut up, boy. This is thick bacon. It takes a while to cook just right. Now, what did you want to talk about?"

Hesitating, Donavan wondered if he should bring this stuff up. He didn't want to sound crazy, or worse yet, like he was afraid of something.

Isaac turned the stove off and set several strips of crispy bacon and six grease fried eggs in a plate on the counter. He grabbed a chair from the kitchen table and sat down in front of Donavan. "Spit it out, son. What's bothering you? Are you worried about testifying against Mickey?"

Shaking his head, Donavan told his father, "No, nothing like that." He grabbed the dishtowel off the counter and fumbled around with it, steadying his trembling hands. When he was ready, he looked at his father and told him what was on his mind. "Have you ever seen those programs where people have near death experiences? And when they are brought back to life they say they were in some kind of tunnel with a bright welcoming light?"

"Yeah, I've seen a show or two like that. What about it?"

"Well, I didn't see no bright light."

"Son, what are you talking about?"

"When I died." He shook his head. "I mean, when I almost died." Looking thoughtful for a moment, he continued. "I was in some kind of tunnel alright—but I could tell that this wasn't it for me. I was headed someplace else." He lowered his gaze. "It was dark—dark and hot."

Isaac lifted his eyes to heaven and silently prayed. *Lord, Jesus, please let this be his first and last trip to hell.*

Isaac put his hand on his son's leg. "Do you know where you were?"

When Donavan looked up, droplets of tears were cascading down his young face. "They tortured me, Dad."

Nina poked her head in the kitchen. "Everything okay?"

Isaac waved her back. "Let me take care of this."

Worried, she excused herself and sat back down on the couch in the living room.

Grabbing his son, Isaac hugged him tight—real tight. "You know where you were, don't you son?"

Shaking his head up and down, Donavan continued to sob. "Now I know what you and Mom talk about is true. There is a heaven, but there's also a hell. I don't ever want to see that place again, Dad."

Isaac stood up, took his son by the hand and walked into the living room where Nina was. "I think your mom will want to be a part of this too." He sat his son down, with Nina beside him, and explained the journey toward heaven. When Donavan was ready, Nina was given the honor of reciting the sinner's prayer with their son.

Just after breakfast, but before Isaac could get out of the kitchen and get dressed for the day, someone knocked on the door again. He didn't care if it was a Jehovah's Witness this time, somebody was getting told off. You just don't show up at people's homes early in the morning without calling.

Nina was sitting on the couch. Legs propped up, waiting on him to answer the door. Oh, now she remembers doctor's orders. But when Charlie was here, Isaac couldn't keep her in her seat.

She pointed at his attire. "You might want to change before opening the door again, don't you think?" The belt hung loose as his open robe revealed his chest. It wasn't washboard beautiful, but the boy wasn't nowhere near flab either. His well-toned thighs and legs were more than Nina should have to endure, let alone some unsuspecting visitors.

"These people deserve what they get. Maybe if I answer the door like this, they'll think twice before going over someone else's house early in the morning. Disturbing folks." His hand was on the doorknob when he turned back and smiled at her. "However, if it bothers you to watch a fine brother like me strut through the house, I'll go cover myself right now."

"You don't bother me, Isaac Walker. I don't pay you any attention."

Laughing he said, "Yeah, that's what I thought."

He pulled the door open and his smile turned upside down. The last two people he'd ever want to see were standing in his face grinning. "What do you want?"

Cassandra rushed in and put her arms around Isaac. "Oh, baby, I couldn't stay away any longer. I just had to know how you were doing. And how everything was going with your son."

Donavan picked that moment to drag himself out of the kitchen.

Usually Wrong walked in. Unwanted and undaunted.

Isaac pulled Cassandra's arms from around his neck and addressed his father. "So you're just going to walk up in my house uninvited."

Nina looked at Isaac as if to ask, "When's the last time you paid rent over here?"

"I wanted to see you, son." Marvin's voice held the uncertainty he felt. His eyes were filled with regret.

Clenching his teeth, Isaac told Marvin, "I told you not to call me that."

"Dad, is this your father?" Donavan asked, excitedly.

Marvin turned to look at his grandson. "Yes, I am. And I bet you're Donavan. I've been waiting to meet you."

If Donavan's back didn't still ache from the bullets being pulled out, he would have leaped for joy. At that moment, he didn't look like someone carrying the burden of testifying so that families of Mickey's victims could have some sense of peace. He looked like a kid again.

"Sir, I've wanted to meet you my whole life," Donavan admitted.

Marvin embraced his grandson. Isaac noticed the way they held on tight. Clinging to one another.

Beaming from the couch, Nina said, "I can't believe you're here. We've wanted to meet you for so long."

Marvin released Donavan. Isaac wanted to check his son for fleas.

Nina's outstretched hand greeted Marvin. "I'm Nina Lewis, Donavan's mother."

Isaac was mad. Fuming. He strapped his robe and went outside to stand on the porch. He wanted to throw that imposter out of the house, but he didn't have the heart to hurt Donavan or Nina like that. He could see how much this meeting meant to them. They just didn't know that they were saying cheese and posing for the devil.

The screen door opened and Cassandra came to stand next to him. Nina and Charles. Him and Cassandra. None of it made sense. It didn't feel right to him.

"I'm sorry about what happened in Chicago, Isaac," Cassandra said. She lowered her head, then continued. "I promise you, nothing like that will ever happen again. Just give me another chance. I really think we could be good together."

He turned toward her and leaned against the banister. She

was a pretty enough girl. He liked her long hair and he liked her endearing smile. Loved her voice. But again, it just didn't feel right. Like he was trying to make a round peg fit into a square hole.

"I don't know, Cassandra. Maybe this thing just isn't supposed to happen for us."

"That's not what you said a couple of weeks ago."

"Things change, Cassandra. And to tell you the truth, I've got a lot on my plate right now."

She stepped closer to him. "I understand that, Isaac, and I'm not trying to pressure you. Just don't forget about me. Okay?"

"Sit down right here and tell us about yourself," Nina told Marvin after she watched Cassandra walk out of the house after Isaac. Nina wanted to leave Marvin in the living room with Donavan and go eavesdrop on Isaac's conversation; but she wouldn't stoop that low.

Marvin gently touched his grandson's cheek. "I can't believe Isaac named you after his brother." He sat next to Nina. "But, you know something? You look just like him."

"Really?" Donavan asked with a sparkle in his eyes.

"I tell you what. The next time I come to visit, I'll bring some pictures."

"That would be wonderful, Mr. Walker," Nina pressed. "Now please, tell us what you've been doing these past years."

A look of sadness crossed his eyes. "There isn't much to my life. I've spent most of it just trying to put broken pieces back together."

Nina's heart went out to him. She covered his hand with her own and squeezed. "I'm sure it's been hard for you."

Tears clung to the corners of his eyes. "Not a day goes by that I don't wish I could turn back time."

"Donavan, go get your grandfather some tissue." Nina squeezed Marvin's hand again. "How did you find us?"

"Isaac came to see me about a month ago. Did you know that?"

Nina looked toward the porch. "No. He never told me."

Marvin laughed. "It wasn't his finest hour. He really came to my house to tell me how much he despised me."

Quite different from the reason she kept encouraging Isaac to find his father. "I can believe it."

Marvin turned away from Nina. He stood and walked to her mantle. "I just wish he didn't have so many reasons to hate me. Wish I had been a better father." He turned back to Nina. "That's why I jumped at the chance to come down here when Isaac's fiancé offered to bring me. I wanted to show him that I've changed. I'm not the same man he once knew."

After the word fiancé, the rest of Marvin's conversation sounded a lot like blah, blah, blah. "Isaac's engaged?" Nina asked while looking more curious than she wanted to, but she couldn't help herself.

"When did my dad get engaged," Donavan asked when he walked back into the room on the tail end of the conversation.

Marvin looked from Nina to Donavan with an oops-I-spilled-the-beans look on his face. "I'm sorry, I thought you knew."

# 33

Now he was supposed to sit down and break bread with a man he couldn't stand, and a woman he hoped to never see again. All Nina's idea of course.

Pizzas for everybody 'cause he wasn't cooking jack. Wouldn't even burn a piece of toast or run water for some Kool-Aid. Let 'em dehydrate.

"What do you think we should fix for lunch, Isaac?" Nina looked at him stiffly.

"I have no idea, Nina." *See what you can fix with that sling on your arm.*

"I know. I know. Let's get some pizza," Donavan said, all excited as if they were getting ready to have a pajama party.

"Okay, pizza it is." Nina turned to Isaac again and smiled sweetly. "Isaac, would you mind going to Donatos to get us a couple of pizzas?"

"Don't think my car will make the trip all the way over to Main Street," Isaac told Nina.

"What are you talking about, Isaac? You drive that car to Chicago and back," Nina said. Isaac gave her a hard stare down. Nina rolled her eyes at Isaac and then turned to her son and asked, "Donavan, can you call Pizza Hut and order a couple of pizzas?"

The pizzas arrived within thirty minutes. All the wanted and unwanted guests sat at the dining room table to eat. Conversation was stilted around the table. Isaac was mad at Nina and hateful to his father. So, he sat with Cassandra on one side and Donavan on the other. Cassandra kept leaning into him, rubbing his shoulder and squeezing his hand.

Nina spent more time biting her lip than biting into her Supreme pan pizza. She was furious with Isaac for not telling her about this woman.

Isaac whispered something in Cassandra's ear. Her head fell back, long black hair flowing, as she laughed.

Picking up a mushroom that fell off her pizza, Nina asked Cassandra, "So, have you and Isaac set a date for your wedding yet?"

A sausage lodged in Isaac's throat and he almost choked. Cassandra hit him on his back a couple times as she told Nina, "Not yet, but I'm hoping that will come soon."

Isaac picked up his glass of water and gulped it down.

Nina looked directly at Isaac. "Well, until you actually get married, I don't think you should be clinging to this woman in front of your son. At least, not in my house."

Cassandra scooted a little to the right. No longer rubbing elbows with Isaac, she gave Nina a scowling glare.

Isaac slammed his glass down. "I'm not clinging to anybody."

Nina rolled her eyes and harrumphed. "She has been rubbing and squeezing on you since we sat down to eat. My God, Isaac, it's obscene."

Isaac pushed his plate away and stood. He was angry, as he pointed at Nina. "You've got a lot of nerve sitting over there judging me. Judge yourself," he told her and stalked off.

"What's that supposed to mean," Nina asked, getting out of her seat. She looked awkward trying to follow behind Isaac with that sling on her arm and her slow hesitant walk, but she did her best.

Looks were exchanged around the table.

Isaac stopped in the living room. He was fuming, but he didn't want Nina to hurt herself trying to keep up with him. "Sit down, Nina. Sit down and mind your own business."

She ignored him. "What do I need to judge myself about, Isaac?"

"Okay, I'll tell you. How do you think Donavan took it this morning when you were all huddled up with Charles at the front door?"

She gasped. "I was not."

This time Isaac harrumphed.

"You haven't bothered to say two words to your father." Nina pointed into the dining room where Cassandra, Marvin and Donavan wisely chose to stay. "That man traveled all the way from Chicago to see you."

"I didn't ask that wife beater to come here. I would have thrown him out, but as you informed me, this is your house."

Nina gasped again. "Isaac Walker, at this very moment, I am ashamed of you." She sat on the couch and turned her face from him.

An awkward silence filled the room. Isaac's heart beat violently inside his chest. Usually Wrong was the cause of all this. If he had stayed where he was wanted, none of this would have happened. He wanted to go back to the dining room and beat that old man like he stole something—'cause he had. He'd stolen Isaac's youth, his mother, his brother and a whole host of other things Isaac couldn't think of right now.

Feeling the rage boiling in him again, Isaac clenched his fist as his jaw tightened. He closed his eyes and sunk into the realization that no matter how much Jesus he possessed, a part of him still carried the root of anger and bitterness. Nothing he could do about it, it was just there. Then Isaac remembered that God's Word says that when he is tempted, God would make a way of escape for him.

His eyes sprung open with the realization. "Life is about choices."

"What?" Nina asked without looking his way.

"Nothing," Isaac responded while looking for his way of escape. "I'm going out for awhile. I'll be back."

As Isaac swung open the screen door, Cassandra ran after him. "I'm coming with you, Isaac. Wait up."

"I'm sorry," Marvin said, as he and Donavan joined Nina in the living room. "I didn't mean to cause problems by bringing Cassandra here with me."

Nina waved her hand dismissively. "I'm not upset about her."

Marvin looked at her suspiciously. "You sure?"

"Yeah, yeah. Isaac just needs to learn some respect." She dismissed Marvin's comment, but her thought, nonetheless, betrayed her. Her knees became weak with memories.

*They had met at a nightclub. She still remembered how the honey oozed out of Isaac's chocolate-coated mouth as he asked, "Have you been waiting long?"*

*She looked into those deep chestnut eyes. Eyes that seemed to read her every thought and intent. Lord have mercy. "Waiting for what?"*

*"A man. Someone to take care of you, like you deserve."*

*I'm still waiting, Isaac,* Nina said within herself. She turned her face from Marvin as she wiped away the lone tear that trickled down her cheek.

# 34

Memories plagued Isaac also. Nina was the only woman that had stuck to his soul. The one he wanted. But he had never measured up in her sight. They just couldn't get the dance right. It still hurt when he thought about that night so many years ago, when he came to her practically on bended knee.

*"You're carrying my baby—you belong with me," Isaac had said to Nina.*

*She looked down at her hands. "We're not married."*

*Isaac opened the closet and threw her clothes onto the bed. "I don't know what these people have been filling your head with, but," he said, pointing at her belly, "that's mine. And that makes you and me family." Nina had started attending church and Isaac believed that the church was turning her against him.*

*Nina had opened her mouth and told him, "I will not live with you."*

*Kneeling down in front of her, Isaac tilted her head toward him so he could look into her eyes. She was sad, he could tell that right off. But there was something else in those eyes, something he hadn't noticed before. Was it peace? No, no, maybe it was conviction he'd seen. Or maybe it was both. He couldn't be sure at the time, but there had definitely been something different about her.*

*"You know I don't want nobody but you," he'd said while rubbing her shoulders. "It's you and me against the world. Come on, baby, come home with me. Please."*

*She put her hands to her face as a tear fell to her cheek. "I can't live in your world anymore. I don't belong there."*

*Isaac had jumped up, agitated. Beg mode over. "Where do you belong, if not with me, huh?"*

*Nina flinched, but said nothing.*

*"Girl, who do you think will treat you better than I have? Look around." He grabbed the clothes off the bed and flung them on the floor. "You happy in these Salvation Army rags? I kept you in Gucci and St. John's. Whatever you wanted, all you had to do was ask. What other man do you think can afford you? Shoot, truth be told, Nina, I barely can."*

*Silence.*

*Isaac strutted around the room. Anger magnified. "I've done everything you asked me to do, so what's the problem?" he'd yelled.*

*No matter what he had done to her through the years— no matter how angry he had made her, he could always look into her eyes and see how much she loved him. But as she looked at him at that very moment, and their eyes locked, he'd found no love for him there. "Nina, don't you know how much I care about you?"*

*Nina softly said, "If you care for me, let me go."*

*He was a man. He could take just about anything, but to look into those sad eyes everyday and know that she had stopped loving him was more than he ever wanted to en-*

*dure. He turned away from those unloving eyes and sur-*
*rendered. "Fine, stay here. Rot here if you like, I don't*
*care."*

Isaac knew one thing for sure. Nina was the same yesterday, today and forever. Whether he was living for the Lord or
running the streets, she wanted nothing to do with him.
She'd told him that she couldn't live in his world. Now, Cassandra was a different matter all together. He could have her
if he wanted. She'd made that abundantly clear. But he was
closed for business and not taking applications anytime
soon. It was late when Isaac and Cassandra pulled up in
front of Nina's house. Marvin and Nina were sitting on the
porch. Isaac was at least thankful that Usually Wrong hadn't
driven back to Chicago without Cassandra.

Nina came toward Isaac with her hand on her hip and her
finger waging. "Isaac, do you know that you've been gone
for three hours?"

Isaac hunched his shoulders. "I was driving around.
What's the big deal?"

Still waging her finger in his face, she told him, "The big
deal is, Marvin needs to get back to Chicago to tend to his
family and he couldn't leave without Cassandra since he
brought her here."

Angry, Isaac said, "Don't tell me about his family." Isaac
pointed a finger at Marvin as he stepped off the porch to join
them on the sidewalk. "He destroyed his family when he
murdered my mother."

Marvin held up his hands and continued walking toward
them. "I don't want you and Nina arguing over me. I'm leaving. I was just waiting on you to get back with Cassandra. I
didn't want you to have to drive all the way to Chicago to
drop her off."

"I don't need your help," Isaac said. His anger was making

him so illogical that he was willing to drive Cassandra all the way to Chicago to avoid letting his father do anything for him.

"How do you know what we need?" Nina challenged. She was angry, reckless and just flat out didn't care tonight. "You run off with Cassandra and leave us here to fend for ourselves. I'm grateful that your father was kind enough to stick around. Somebody had to see about me and Donavan, because we sure needed help."

"I drove around with Cassandra." He was screaming at Nina. "I knew you didn't want her here, so I drove all around town just to keep her out of your face. My God, what do you want from me?"

Nina stole a quick glance at Cassandra. Cassandra put her hand on Isaac's arm. Tension was thick, but no one said anything.

Marvin took that moment to hug Nina and thank her for allowing him to visit with his grandson. "I've got to get home to my wife and children."

"How many times have you beaten her since you've been married?" Isaac asked with hatred in his eyes.

Marvin turned sad haunted eyes on Isaac. "Son—"

"Don't call me that," Isaac demanded.

Marvin continued. "You may never forgive me for what I did, but I want you to know that I am truly sorry for how I destroyed my family. Your mother was a good woman. But I was drunk all the time back then, so I just didn't notice how good she was. I haven't taken a drink in fifteen years."

Isaac put his hands in his pocket, trying his best not to get any angrier than he already was. He had a choice. *Choose not to fight, Isaac. Choose what God would want.*

"I'm going to get out of your way," Marvin told him. His eyes were swimming in a pool of liquid matter. "I know you don't need a father anymore. You're all grown up. But if you should need a friend, someone to talk to, give me a call."

*With friends like him, Isaac would call Mickey first.*

Nina put her arm on Marvin's shoulder as he turned to walk away. She glared back at Isaac like he was the villain here. Like he was the one who'd killed somebody's mama instead of the other way around. She needed to be glaring at the one she was consoling—*watch out for his left hook.*

Cassandra turned to Isaac and asked, "When do you think you'll be back in Chicago?"

Isaac looked over at Nina. The sling was still on her arm. "I'm not sure. But, I'll call and let you know something soon. Okay?"

"Alright. I'll talk to you soon," she said as she walked over to Marvin's car and got in on the passenger side.

When Marvin and Cassandra drove off, Nina marched back into the kitchen to finish this fight once and for all. "You should be ashamed of yourself, Isaac Walker."

"Is Donavan sleep?" Isaac asked Nina.

"Yes, of course he's sleep. It's eleven at night." Nina's hand was back on her hip.

"That sounds like a plan. Goodnight, Nina, I need to get some rest."

"Oh, no, Isaac. We are going to finish this conversation."

"Not tonight. I'm tired and I'm going to bed," Isaac told her as he walked up the stairs and into his bedroom, leaving Nina standing in the living room with her mouth hanging open. Aimlessly driving around town had whupped on Isaac, so he fell out on the bed with his street clothes on.

The next morning, Isaac was feeling a bit repentant. So he rose early and set about making pancakes for everyone. His first two batches burned. He had stirred the new mix and put more batter in the skillet when Nina walked into the kitchen. She had taken the sling off her arm. She held her arm close to her body as she opened the refrigerator and poured herself a glass of juice.

Pointing at her arm, Isaac asked, "Why'd you take it off?"

"It's time," was all Nina said as she put the juice back in the refrigerator.

"What's that supposed to mean?" Her words irritated him because they were the same words she'd spoken to him the night he dreamed about her coming to him. The night she and Donavan got shot.

She turned to face him. "Time for life to be normal again. Time for me to fluff my own pillows and cook my own meals. Time for you to go home."

He placed the bowl down on the counter and glared at her. "So, it's like that, huh?"

Tension clung to the air as they stood their ground, neither yielding. Both seeing their own stubborn reality and getting it wrong.

"Whatever," he said when Nina wouldn't respond. He scooped the pancakes off the skillet.

Nina turned to him then and let him have it. "You're supposed to be a Christian, Isaac. If you can't forgive others, what makes you so sure that God can continue to forgive all the mess you get yourself into?"

Pointing the spatula in her face, he said, "You need to take your own advice."

"What are you talking about?" She was screaming. Just couldn't take him one second longer.

Ignoring the temper tantrum, he said, "You spout off about forgiving everybody under the sun. You released Mickey for shooting you, and Charles for dumping you. But you haven't forgiven me, Nina. I don't care how much you claim it."

"I have." The sneer could be heard in her voice from here to Alabama.

"Then why do you hold me hostage to the things of the past? You won't let me close to you. Won't even consider a future with me, and I know why."

She just glared at him.

"You don't trust me. And the reason you don't trust me is because you haven't forgiven me."

"Like I said, I forgave you a long time ago." Her words were tight and drawn out.

Isaac leaned against the kitchen counter and shook his head. "No. Not completely. I believe that you forgave some of the things that I did to you. But the one thing you still hold onto is the women. You don't think I would be faithful to you. Admit it, Nina."

She laughed. "Do you even know the definition? How can I believe you would be faithful when you're always flaunting your women in front of me? Don't think I've forgotten how you used to tell me that your other girlfriends were my wife-in-laws."

Of all the things he wished he could take back, those words would be on the top ten. He'd hurt her when he spouted off that nonsense. But he had been young and stupid. "Look, Nina, I'm sorry that I ever said that to you. But I haven't flaunted a woman in front of you in years."

"What about Cassandra?"

Okay, maybe he did let Cassandra rub on his shoulders and squeeze his hand just to tick Nina off. But he had been mad about her huddled conversation with Charles. "I didn't ask Cassandra to come here. I know you're not mad at me for dating someone. Don't forget, you were engaged."

She shook her head, calming down. "I'm not upset about you dating. Your women just always seem to end up on my doorstep."

"I'm sorry about that too." It seemed like he was always apologizing to this woman, but this time he really was sorry. He knew the incident Nina was referring to. His old girl-friend, Denise, had followed him to Dayton one weekend. After he picked up Donavan and headed back to Chicago, she knocked on Nina's door. Denise hoodwinked Nina into believing that she was pregnant. Begged Nina to help convince Isaac to marry her. The girl was no more pregnant than he was. That's when he stopped fornicating. To this day, he wasn't sure if he left Denise alone for God or because of how hurt Nina sounded when she tried to convince him to marry another woman.

She waved off his compassion. "It doesn't matter anymore. I'm just tired of dealing with you and your women."

They stood staring at each other, silence eating up the minutes. Isaac's cell phone rang and he leaped on it. "Yeah?"

"Hey, Isaac, my boy. How are things going?" It was Bishop Sumler.

"Not too good, Bishop. How are things going with you?" Isaac asked in a voice that sounded as if he hadn't had a good night's sleep in weeks and was about to collapse at any moment.

Bishop didn't seem to notice as he got right to the point. "That's why I'm calling. There are a few things going on here that could use your attention."

"Can Keith work on it?"

Bishop hesitated for a moment and then said, "I have Keith working on some other things. I really need you here if you can get away."

Isaac looked at Nina's arm again, the one that had a sling on it, before she removed it to prove to him that she didn't need him. The look of sadness in her eyes told him that she wanted him out of her hair so he told Bishop, "All right. I'll be there."

Isaac hung up the phone and turned back to Nina. "Well, I guess you got your wish. I might not be needed here anymore, but Bishop needs me back in Chicago."

"Yeah, Bishop always seems to need you," Nina mumbled.

"What did you say?"

Nina didn't back down, she rolled her eyes heavenward and said, "That man means you no good. He knows you've got all these anger and unforgiveness issues—and what does he do about it? Does he pray for you; try to guide you in the right direction? No, your Bishop uses you as his henchman. He feeds on your anger issues and lets you do all of his dirty work."

"I'm no body's henchman," Isaac said angrily.

Nina squeezed her eyes shut and then reopened them. "All right, fine. I've said what I've wanted to tell you about that man for some time now. But if you don't believe what is so very obvious, then I can't help you. Go to Chicago, Isaac. It's for the best."

"I don't need your permission," he told her as he walked out of the kitchen. He turned back around and said more compassionately, "I'll take Donavan with me so you don't have to worry about taking care of him and yourself."

"That's fine. When will you bring him back?"

"A couple of days." He turned and headed for his son's room.

A tear trickled down her face. "Run away like you always do."

# 35

Isaac was in an uncomfortable place. He sat in Bishop Sumler's office thinking over his life and his ministry. Everything was up in the air. He had been praying, asking God to direct him. But he still didn't know which end was up, or where he was going from here.

He believed, deep in his heart, that God had forgiven him for his transgressions—the rest of the world may never, but God had. He believed he was still called of God, still meant to do something. He just didn't know what it was. He also thought about what Nina had said about Bishop Sumler using him as a henchman and that he wasn't able to get rid of his issues because of continued association with Bishop. *Lord, could this be true?*

Sumler greeted Isaac jovially as he rushed into his office. "Sorry I'm late. Putting out a fire on the other side of town."

Isaac knew all about the fires Bishop put out. He'd done the same for him when he'd gotten himself caught up with Denise. Isaac still wondered how much that New York relocation had cost Bishop.

Sumler sat behind his desk and fumbled around for some papers. "Isaac, my boy, I think it is your time."

Nina had just told him it was time for him to leave her house. He wondered what time Bishop thought it was, but didn't ask.

"I've got two churches that do not have a full-time pastor. The one in West Virginia and one here." Bishop looked at Isaac and smiled. "What I want to know is, which one do you want to start your career as a pastor in?"

Isaac wanted to jump out of his seat and shout hallelujah. About time something good occurred in his life. But something kept him in his seat. Maybe it was the way Bishop called preaching a career. Wasn't it supposed to be a ministry? Or maybe it was the memory of Pastor Paul reaching out to people most of Christendom had given up on. Wasn't that what this walk was supposed to be about?

"I would love to pastor a church, sir. I just don't know if this is the right time for me. I've been going through some things. So I've been seeking God about what I'm supposed to do next."

"It's time to stop seeking and become a doer. This is what God has for you. I feel it in my bones."

Rubbing his chin, Isaac pondered. Taking over one of the churches sounded good to him. It was why he'd sat under Bishop all these years. He really didn't understand why he was hesitating. *God is this you? Or are you pulling me in another direction?* "Let me pray about it a little while and discuss it with my family."

Bishop Sumler's brows rose. "What family, son?"

"Nina and Donavan," he said flatly. Nina was acting a fool right now, but that didn't take away from the value he placed on her opinion. Isaac still held himself responsible for Donavan getting mixed up with the wrong crowd. He was determined to be there for his family, no matter the cost.

Sumler put his elbow on his desk and leaned in closer to Isaac. "Son, I've been meaning to talk to you about this for quite some time." He hesitated, then just threw it out there. "You need a wife."

*Not this conversation again.* At least three times a year, Bishop got on this "Isaac, you need a wife" kick and Isaac was getting tired of it. "I'd love to have a wife, Bishop. I just haven't interviewed too many acceptable applicants lately."

"I'm gon' be honest with you." Bishop got up and walked around his desk. "If you leave that gal in Dayton alone, you might find a wife a whole lot sooner."

"What's Nina got to do with anything?" Isaac asked, the look on his face daring the Bishop to say anything against the mother of his child.

Bishop raised his hands. "Calm down, son. All I'm saying is, she's not for you. She's not ministry material like some of these other women I've sent your way."

It wasn't right to laugh in the face of a man of God. Isaac tried to contain himself. But Bishop was living in some kind of la-la land if he thought the women he'd introduced him to were ministry material.

"Don't get me wrong, Nina's a nice enough girl, but she doesn't sing. She won't be able to draw in the crowd you'll need."

Isaac did laugh now. "Bishop, I'll take a prayer warrior over a soloist any day."

Bishop Sumler walked over to Isaac and put his hands on his shoulder. "Son, stop sleeping with that girl and come on back home where you belong."

Isaac jumped out of his seat and once again reminded himself that anger was an emotion, violence was a choice. But the fact that he was puffed up with anger and Bishop didn't seem all that bothered by it, didn't go unnoticed by Isaac. He unclenched his fist and stepped away from the man of God. "Bishop, that wasn't called for. Nina is not like that."

Sumler held up his hands. "Relax, Isaac. I'm just looking out for your own good. You've got a great future ahead of you. I just don't want you to mess it up doing something stupid."

"Well you don't have to worry about that. Because it's like I said, Nina doesn't do that kind of stuff." He wanted to add, *unlike the women you hook me up with,* but he left that one alone.

Directing Isaac to the door, Bishop told him, "Go home and pray about this. See what the Lord has to say about you earning millions of dollars a year."

Isaac couldn't help himself. A million dollar announcement would make anybody do a double take. He almost stumbled over his words as he asked, "The church wouldn't pay me a million a year, would it?"

Bishop shook his head. "No, no. You'd start out earning about a hundred thousand. But with the books you'll write and being on the preaching circuit, you'll pull in a million easy."


"I feel so alone, Elizabeth. Nobody wants to be around me," Nina said as she held the telephone to her ear.

"That's not true, Nina."

Nina sat down on the couch with her feet underneath her bottom and continued to sulk. "Charles and I would still be engaged if I could have children."

"Nina, please don't take this the wrong way, because I know you're hurting. But would you really want to marry a man that places conditions on his love?"

"No, I don't want Charles." She unfolded her legs, stretched out on the couch and sighed. "I don't know what I want. I probably wouldn't even be thinking about Charles if they hadn't left me."

"Who left you?"

"Keep up with me, Elizabeth. I'm talking about Donavan and Isaac."

"What do they have to do with Charles?"

"Well, if they were still here, I wouldn't be thinking about Charles. But Isaac ran back to Chicago to his girlfriend."

Elizabeth sighed heavily. "Nina, you put the man out!"

"Yeah, right. Nobody can just put Isaac Walker out. If he wanted to stay, he would have refused to leave."

"Nina, as long as I've known you, Isaac has been bending over backward to be with you." She switched the phone from one ear to the other. "Now, I understand why you wanted nothing to do with him when he was dealing drugs, but he's saved now. The man loves the Lord."

Nina laughed. "He just tried to kill someone, Elizabeth."

"I hate to break it to you, Nina, but I wanted to kill that animal."

"But you didn't."

"Neither did Isaac."

Nina harrumphed. "He tried."

"Bottom line," Elizabeth said, firmly, "what do you want to do?"

Nina had moped around the house for two days. She wished Donavan had stayed. She'd then have something to take her mind off the empty hole Isaac's absence left. Now she was on the phone with Elizabeth and her best friend was asking her what she wanted to do. Didn't she know that life was more complicated than that?

She gripped the phone and cried, "I don't know what I want."

"Yes, you do," Elizabeth's patient voice sang through the receiver.

Nina grabbed some tissue and blew her nose. "You can't always have what you want. Sometimes, it's not good for you."

"Look, Nina, let's cut to the chase. I know that you're in

love with Isaac. What I don't understand is why you won't give him a chance."

She started to deny that love-fest thing Elizabeth was talking about. Isaac was all wrong for her—too dangerous. She needed someone stable, someone reliable, someone without issues. But in truth, her heart belonged to the man who admitted to her that he was dealing with demons. How twisted was that?

# 36

Isaac picked up a pizza from Gino's, and he and Donavan went back to his apartment. He desperately needed somebody to talk to. Needed to reason this thing out. Isaac just wasn't sure if it was God's will for him to accept the pastoral position Bishop Sumler offered him. Keith was all for the idea. Thought it was the right thing to do. Of course he did. Keith wanted the associate pastor position. Isaac was all right with taking the job as well. He just couldn't figure out why his spirit was in such turmoil.

His father had told him that if he needed a friend, he could talk to him. That was laughable. Isaac would rather take his chances with Nina's rage.

He picked up the phone, hesitated, then dialed her number. The air conditioner was out in his apartment. Donavan was complaining about the heat. So while Nina was saying hello, Isaac opened the living room window. "Hey, how's it going?" Isaac asked.

Silence.

He pleaded. "I really need a friend right now, Nina. Can I talk to you?"

"I'm a little busy right now, Isaac. I'm trying to finish my book. My editor has been calling for it."

Donavan yelled, "Hi, Mom," loud enough for Nina to hear him, then he laughed, and pointed at his dad. "Ha, ha, ha. She got you begging like a dog."

"Shut up, boy. Go clean up that mess you made in the kitchen." He shoved Donavan out of the room and pressed the phone back to his ear. "I really need to talk to you."

"Tell Donavan I miss him," Nina said, then she asked Isaac with a bit of spite in her voice, "Where is Cassandra?"

"Come on, Nina. I don't want that woman. You know how I feel."

"Talk."

Isaac heard the coldness of her voice, but he didn't care. His need was stronger than his pride. Numerous times, in years gone by, she had needed him. He always treated her with cool indifference. "Bishop offered me a pastoral position at either the church in West Virginia or the one here in Chicago."

"And?"

"Well, I could earn a boat load of money. We would be set. You know. We wouldn't have the money issues we have right now."

"I hear a 'but' somewhere, Isaac. What's wrong with the offer?"

He hunched his shoulders. "I don't know. I'm having a hard time getting a 'yes' from my spirit on this one."

"If you don't feel right about the offer, turn it down."

"It's not that simple, Nina. This is a whole lot of money to just walk away from. And how do I know this is not God's will for my life?"

"Have you prayed about it yet?"

He switched the phone from one ear to the other. "Can I come home, Nina? Can we pray about this together?"

"You don't live here, Isaac."

"You know what I mean." Through his open window he could hear Otis Redding singing, *"I've been loving you a little too long—I don't wanna stop now."* Nina heard it too. He knew it from the way the line went dead silent. She was feeling Otis. A memory of their first slow dance trickled through his mind. Was she thinking about that too? "I need to be there with you, Nina. This is an important decision. I don't want to make it alone."

*With you my life has been so wonderful—I can't stop now.*

"I'll wait up for you. We'll pray when you get here," Nina told him, then hung up the phone.

# 37

The door opening at Nina's house felt good. Felt like coming home. She stood there looking at him as he and Donavan walked in. *It's me, baby. The one you were born to love,* Isaac wanted to say, but he chose the safer route. "Thanks for letting us come back."

Nina hugged Donavan. "Hey, boy. I missed you."

"We were only gone two days," he told her, then smiled. "I missed you too."

"You better had." She swiped him on the butt. "Go take a bath and get ready for bed."

"Just what I was thinking." Donavan saluted his parents. "Goodnight, folks."

Nina turned to Isaac. "Are you ready to pray?"

"Oh, I almost forgot. I'll be right back," Isaac said as he ran out of the house.

Nina stood at the door with her arms folded and her foot tap, tap, tapping. Her eyes and posture said it all. She was still upset with Isaac and his forgetting something outside didn't endear him to her at all.

However, when Isaac walked back in the door with the

boutique of lilies he'd left in the car and said, "I brought a peace offering," Nina's face softened. "I just wanted you to know how sorry I am for all the drama I caused before Donavan and I left the other day." He offered her the lilies. "I know they're your favorite."

Nina unfolded her arms and took the lilies from Isaac. "Thanks, Isaac." She headed toward the kitchen as she told him, "Go on into the living room, I'll get a vase and put my lilies in it and then we can pray."

"All right," Isaac said, adding, "Oh, and Nina." Nina stopped and turned. "Thanks for letting me come back."

Nina couldn't stay mad at Isaac. He was adorable when he was repentant. She smiled at him and truthfully said, "I'm glad you came back."

Nina put her flowers in a vase and then she and Isaac knelt in the living room. Their hands joined as they united in prayer. Isaac began their petition. "Father, we come to you tonight, humbled by your greatness and your wisdom. For you, oh Lord, have the answer to all our situations. Your Word says that there are many plans in a man's heart, but the end thereof is destruction. I don't want to plot and plan my life to gain riches and destroy myself in the process. Help me make the right decision, Lord. Lead me and guide me into your perfect will."

When Isaac finished, Nina took over. "Lord, we ask that you bring the people in Isaac's path that he needs to associate himself with. He loves you, Lord. I believe that with all my heart. Help him to walk upright before you in all his dealings. If taking this pastoral job is an opportunity from you, then I pray that you speak to him directly about it. Guide him, Father. For your way is the only way to eternal life. In Jesus' name we pray and believe that we will know your perfect will in this situation."

They stood and hugged as people normally do in church

after someone prays for them. But this wasn't church, so they lingered just a bit longer in each other's arms.

Nina backed away first. "I'll see you in the morning. God will speak to your heart, Isaac. I'll keep praying. Okay?"

He reached out and grabbed her hand. He needed to hold onto her for a moment longer. "Thanks, Nina."

Averting her eyes, she replied, "You're welcome. Goodnight, I'm going to bed."

After Nina went to her bedroom, Isaac climbed the stairs to his bedroom with the realization that although Nina was gone from his presence, she was not gone from his heart, his thoughts, or his longings. He'd die loving that woman.

As he got into bed, his body ached from all the traveling he'd done. Closing his eyes, Isaac prayed that God would show Himself. But, only he could pray for God and meet up with the devil. He was on another journey back to hell and was powerless to stop this descent.

Sweat trickled down Isaac's forehead. The heat was unbearable. Potholes of fire bubbled under his feet. The place was just as Isaac remembered. The air was gaseous, polluted, dry and tainted. Truth had once told him that it was the smell of death, decay and dying that greeted the inhabitants of hell. Isaac was alone this trip. Truth was nowhere in sight. But that wasn't really factual, because truth now resided within him. That fact alone energized Isaac.

"Might as well start walking." Isaac was sure that he wasn't getting out of there, until he saw whatever he was supposed to see while down there. Scream after agonizing scream penetrated his soul and made him cover his ears and shrink back. Blood oozed down the walls of the tunnel of death. Isaac wanted to close his eyes so he wouldn't have to witness the pain and destruction, but there was no such thing as a closed eye in hell. It was as if his eyes were permanently glued open. The punishment for coming to hell, after having so many chances to accept God, was not only the personal pain inflicted upon a person, nor was watching as others being tortured the worst thing about this place. The worst thing about being an inhabitant of a place like hell was knowing that there is a place of peace that would forever be off limits.

Rejected and tormented souls were encased in the walls of the tunnel, anguishing their misery, as their silhouettes attempted to pierce through the muck and mire. Isaac desperately searched for an opening, but the tunnel was endless. With each turn, he was accosted by another tortured soul trying to pull its way out of the muck.

"Why didn't you tell us," the silhouettes demanded of him over and over again.

"Tell you what? I don't even know you," Isaac screamed at the voices.

"Why didn't you tell us about Jesus?"

Isaac turned and looked in the face of Ton-Ton, a street hustler he had worked with back in the day. Ton-Ton had been tough. He didn't take no mess. Isaac still remembered the Christmas massacre that earned Ton-Ton a ticket to death row.

He turned and gasped as another hustler, who'd died in the game, accused him of neglect.

"Why didn't you tell us about Jesus?" More silhouettes pulled through the muck and showed their faces.

"My God." He remembered them all. Each one had died on the streets without knowing Jesus.

"Why didn't you tell us," they chanted again and again.

"I didn't know about Him when I knew you guys. All of you died before I accepted the Lord," Isaac told them.

Another face pulled through the muck. It was JC. Agony stretched across his face. "Why didn't you tell me? I looked up to you."

Isaac recalled talking against JC to Donavan. *"That boy is a thug. He'll never amount to anything.*" He'd told his son to stop hanging around him. Never once had Isaac gone out of his way to tell JC about God and His redeeming power. He fell down on his knees in the midst of his accusers and cried out, "Oh, Lord, forgive me. I got comfortable preaching in churches. Delivering your Word to people who don't even want the truth, and I forgot about these people."

When Isaac awoke, he was sprawled out on the floor. His threshing floor. His sorrow was evident through his tears. In travail, he lamented for the people he had left behind. "If you are truly the God your Word says you are, then show me Your glory. Speak to my heart. Tell me what you want me to do."

A soft wind blew by him, but God was not in the wind. Thunder roared outside his window. No revelation came to him from that either. But as he continued to lie on the floor, with his mind made up to wait on God, he heard a still soft voice.

*Isaac, my son. You have found favor in my sight. You have ministered to my people, and you have loved my Word; but I have something against you.*

Isaac had taken numerous trips to hell. He'd witnessed his brother's torment and held the knowledge that he could do nothing about it. He'd even fought with demons—in the natural and supernatural. But hearing the actual voice of God was no everyday occurrence for him. He was awed, bowled over by this new thing in his life. He thought he already knew why God was displeased with him. He thought God was upset because of that Glock he was holding a couple of weeks ago. But this was no time for guesswork. He kept his face to the ground. "Speak, Lord. What have I done?"

*You forgot your first love.*

Isaac sat up and leaned against his bed with his head in

his hands. Had he heard wrong? "Lord, you know that my first love was the streets. Your Word told me to come out from among them, so that's what I tried to do."

*Go back.*

Isaac wanted to be obedient, but he was weak in that area. All he could remember was standing over Mickey, contemplating killing him and stealing his drugs.

*I am stronger than your strongman. I will be with you.*

For hours after God's declaration, Isaac lay on the floor praying and crying. He would stand in the gap for the hustlers, pimps, and thieves of the world. This was his assignment from the Lord. He was not meant to pastor a multi-million dollar church or collect honorariums from speaking engagements. God showed him that he was a street preacher.

He wallowed on the floor a while longer, praying that the end of this journey would not find his soul in hell. But if he did not do the will of God, where would his soul find rest? "I'll go, Lord. Send me."

# 38

When Isaac arose from prayer, the moon had descended and the sun ruled the day once again. As he got off the floor, he looked to heaven. "The law of your mouth is better to me than thousands of coins of gold and silver." The words from Psalm 119 wouldn't let Isaac go, so he had surrendered to them.

He opened the bedroom door and walked into the kitchen. Nina was at the stove, putting on a pot of grits. Donavan was sitting at the table.

Nina gazed at Isaac with longing in her heart. They were still. Saying nothing, meaning everything.

Isaac broke the silence. "I'm not going to take the job Bishop offered me."

Donavan's head popped up. "Are you crazy, Dad? Didn't the man offer you a million dollars?"

Isaac held up his hands. "He only said that it was possible to make a million. The church would only pay about a hundred thousand."

"Hello, middle class. Goodbye ghetto. I'm tired of living in this neighborhood anyway," Donavan told him.

Isaac laughed. "This neighborhood is my assignment."

Nina gave him a questioning look as she grabbed a spoon out of the utensil draw and stirred the grits.

What could he say? He was tired of trying to relate his hell experiences to people. Nina would probably understand, but Donavan . . .

"Last night, God spoke to me. I'm supposed to minister to people that are on the street. The same streets I wanted to forget all about." A smile of pride overtook his face as he looked at Nina. "But you didn't forget. No, you never let our past go or forgot that people are hurting on these streets. That's what your writing is all about."

Nina's mouth hung open. "You've read my books? You never mentioned it."

Laughing again, he told her, "Of course I read your books. Can't wait for the next one. And don't think I don't know that Johnson Smalls is me. Just be glad that I can't testify against my own wife."

"Wife?" Donavan and Nina said in unison.

He looked to Donavan. "Shut up, boy. This is grown folks business." Turning his attention back to Nina he said, "You heard me." He strutted over to her, took the spoon out of her hand and looked deep into her hazel eyes. "We were meant to be together, Nina. God put us together from the beginning. I need you, baby. Will you please marry me?"

She tried to speak. He put a finger over her lips.

"Now, when we first got together, we weren't saved, nor thinking about the Lord. I had tons of money and could give you anything you wanted. I don't have that kind of money anymore. And I don't know what the future holds. I can't give you guarantees of riches. But, I can guarantee you that my life, now and forever, is submitted to God."

Tears creased her eyes. "It's never been about the money, Isaac. I-I . . ."

He wiped her tears with his hands and covered her mouth with his lips. Lips that said, "I love you, girl. Can't make it without you." And with her own lips, Nina responded.

"Oooh!" Donavan yelled and pointed at his mother and father.

Nina broke away from Isaac's hold, picked up the spoon and stirred the grits. "Sit down, Isaac. Breakfast will be done in a minute."

Isaac turned her back around to face him. "You didn't answer my question, Nina. Will you marry me?"

The tears that were only creasing her eyes seconds before were now rolling down her face. Nina shook her head. "I can't give you an answer right now, Isaac." She wiped the tears from her face, then said, "Let me pray about it. I'll give you an answer, but I need to know if this is what God wants me to do."

Isaac could understand that. They had been through a lot in the years that he had known her. Isaac was ashamed of a lot of the things he had done to Nina; especially the time he put his hands on her. He stepped away from Nina, not wanting to pressure her. He grabbed a biscuit out of the pan on the stove and took a bite. "This is enough for me. I've got somewhere to go this morning. I'll probably pick up something on my way."

She stopped stirring. "Where are you going?"

He smiled. She hadn't said "I do." She hadn't actually accepted his proposal for that matter. But she was already wanting to know his comings and goings. He could have pointed this out to her, but decided to let it go. "I'm going to see Mickey this morning."

Nina looked nervous. "Are you sure that's a good idea, Isaac?"

"I'm not sure about a whole lot of things right now, but I think I need to do this. I feel like this is the direction God is sending me in."

"Just don't get yourself arrested before the wedding," Donavan joked.

Isaac headed toward the door. "I'll be back this afternoon."

Nina followed and caught up with him on the porch. "I-Isaac, I don't know if you were serious about what you said in there or not. But you do remember that . . ." she looked down at her feet, "I can't have any more children."

Isaac lifted her chin. Their eyes met. "I'm only going to say this once, Nina. Charles is a fool." He kissed her soft moist lips. "See you when I get back."

# 39

Walking toward the visitor's area, wicked memories reeked havoc on Isaac's mind. Mickey had been fifteen years old when Isaac gave him his first job as a runner.

They met at the BP station on the corner of Salem and Grand. "Help me out, Isaac," Mickey had begged him. "My mom is selling her food stamps to buy dope while me and my sister starve to death. You've got to give me a job. How else are we going to eat?"

Spoony had shown Isaac the ropes when he was a little younger than Mickey was at the time. Isaac thought, why not give the kid a break? Throw him some change so he can eat while his trifflin' mama was firing up her crack pipe. "Okay, kid. Meet me right here every Friday morning around nine." That was the start of it.

At fifteen, Mickey worked harder than any of Isaac's other runners. Most of his other runners were either on crack themselves, or smoking tree-loads of marijuana.

The only problem Isaac had out of Mickey was when he told him to stop selling to his own mother.

Mickey became angry and told Isaac, "Her money spends just as good as anybody else's."

"That's not the point," Isaac had tried to reason with him. "She's your mother."

Mickey's beady little eyes rolled upward. "She's a customer."

Isaac threatened Mickey. "If word gets back to me that you sold another piece of crack to your mother, you are through working for me."

Other than Mickey's mama drama dysfunction, he and Isaac worked well together. Isaac had even given Mickey his own territory before he went off to jail. That piece of territory sprouted into Mickey's crazed need to have it all.

Isaac had taught his protégé well. Maybe Mickey was right when he suggested that Isaac wanted him dead because he was tired of looking at himself.

Taking a seat in the visitation room, Isaac waited for them to bring Mickey out. *What am I supposed to say to this man, Lord?* His anger over what Mickey had done to his family had not totally subsided. But they were going for the death penalty; Mickey would pay the ultimate price for his sins. What was left for Isaac to hold over his head?

Isaac heard the familiar clang of the prison doors opening and closing. Mickey was escorted into the opposite room. They would communicate through a glass divider. "How you doing," Isaac asked when Mickey sat down.

"I've been better. How are things going for you? Is the family doing okay," Mickey asked as if he had nothing to do with any problems Isaac's family had.

"Yeah, Mickey, they're doing fine," Isaac said in a calm, even voice which belied his true happiness concerning Nina and Donavan's state of well being.

Sadness invaded Mickey's eyes and he slumped in his seat. "I'm real sorry about—you know—what I did. I just didn't think they mattered all that much to you. I wouldn't have hurt you for the world, Isaac."

Isaac believed that, in some sick twisted way, Mickey meant what he said. "I'm trying to let the whole thing go, Mickey. I forgive you." Just saying those three simple words—words that Isaac had denied every person who had ever wronged him—sent a wave of peace oscillating through Isaac's very being. He could do this—God's will.

For the first time in a long while, Isaac wished he knew what kind of madness went on in Mickey's childhood to cause his mind to snap. Isaac wished he could have helped rather than been the catalyst that brought him where he was today. "Has any of your family been to see you, Mickey?"

He shrugged. "My crack head mom came out here. She put on a good crocodile tear show, then she asked me to tell her where I keep my money." Mickey sat up in his chair. "I spit on her." He laughed. "Well, I spit on this glass, but she got the message."

Isaac was silent, still trying to figure out what to say to this man.

Mickey snapped his finger as he asked Isaac, "Hey, remember when Ray-Ray tried to take your turf?"

Isaac nodded.

"That fat fool thought he could take some of your turf. Man, I wish I could have seen his face when you came down on him with some of that Black on Black crime."

*This was his chance. Come on, Isaac don't blow it.* "Do you know what I wish?"

"That you would have shot Ray-Ray, instead of Keith coming off like the hero."

Isaac shook his head and let the pain of life show through his eyes. "I wish I could go back to that time. Wish I could have just left it alone like Keith suggested. I wish that Ray-Ray were still alive."

Confusion spread across Mickey's face. "Why would you wish a dumb thing like that?"

"Because, Mickey, hustlers don't get special treatment in the hereafter. If you die in the game, you wake up in hell."

Mickey put his arms behind his head and relaxed. "I live in hell everyday. The hell you speak of would be like a Jamaican vacation."

No sense trying to talk Mickey out of his pleasant hell vacation. He would believe that nonsense until he burst through that great hot tunnel. The agony of life without God—no turning back, no second chances—would convince him that he'd been wrong.

"Mickey, have you ever thought about God and His great love for us?"

"Please man, don't make me cuss you out. God played His last joke on me when He gave me that crack head for a mom."

Isaac thought about his father and his hatred of him. He came to the conclusion this morning that he wasn't the only one who'd experienced tragedy. He had to let it go, and let God work a new thing in his heart. Move on, and quit hating everybody. "Okay, you didn't start out with the best, but God loves you. And He desires only good for you."

"News flash, Isaac. I'm off God's Christmas list."

Isaac wondered if things would have been different had he tried to talk to Mickey about the Lord the day he was released from jail. He was wondering about a lot of things lately. Like, had it really been God's will for him to leave with Bishop Sumler, or had God sent Mickey to him? He had been so busy trying to get away from his former life and trying to become a better person that he didn't think about what Mickey or anyone else like him needed. Looking back over the years that he'd been out of prison, Isaac realized that he hadn't become that much better. Yes, he loved the Lord, but he still harbored so much unforgiveness in his heart. Sighing heavily, Isaac tried again. "God forgives our sins, Mickey."

Mickey waved him off. "Look, man, you might need all that weak kneed bowing down to Jesus stuff to ease your guilt, but I'm all right with who I am."

Isaac stood. "Do you mind if I visit you from time to time?"

"You are welcome anytime. But do me a favor. Leave Jesus on the cross when you step in here."

# 40

Isaac didn't know what to expect from his visit with Mickey, but on a scale of one to ten, he'd call it a disaster. Feeling down and wanting to punish himself even more for the sins of his past, he pulled his car into an empty lot on the corner of Broadway and Riverview where he first started his business. He got out of the car and stood at the corner; the very spot he had proclaimed as his Promised Land. The very place he ruled like he was some kind of god.

Since accepting the Lord into his life, Isaac hated driving by the area. He had hoped and prayed that Nina would move so he never would have a reason to be on this side of town. But maybe this, too, had been in God's plan. Maybe he was supposed to drive by this place and be reminded of the sins of his past.

He knelt on the street he had once ruled. As cars passed by, Isaac received questioning glances, but he was not ashamed. God had been too good to him. God had decided to love Isaac even when he wasn't thinking about the Lord. God had forgiven him when he thought he was beyond re-

demption. "Lord, I give this land back to you. This place will
no longer be a promised land for drug dealers, prostitutes
and thieves. In this place, the kingdom of darkness will
come to know you and your marvelous light. In Jesus' name,
I promise that to you."

When Isaac finished praying, a red Navigator with tinted
windows and spinners rounded the corner. The SUV looked
just like the one Mickey tried to give him about three years
ago. The guy that leaned his head out the window, trying to
see what Isaac was doing, was Johnny Homes. He had been
one of Isaac's runners back in the day, just as Mickey and
Lou had been.

Isaac waved him over, thinking that the car was some sort
of sign from God. Johnny pulled up next to Isaac's car. The
two men clasped hands.

"Ah, man, it is good to see you," Johnny said as he got out
of the car.

Isaac hugged him. "I wondered how things turned out for
you."

"I'm holding it down." Johnny strutted a bit so Isaac could
see his diamond bedecked hands, velour Rocawear jogging
suit and Airforce Ones.

Isaac wanted to tell him that the outer man was looking
good these days. But, what was it like for him late at night?
Could he sleep? "Sit down with me for a minute."

Sitting on the hood of his car, Isaac waited for Johnny to
join him. He looked around at the desecrated land and wondered how one man could solve so great a problem.

The hood of Isaac's car sank in a bit as Johnny joined him.

"You look a little down. I hope you ain't trippin' on that
madness with Mickey," Johnny said.

Isaac looked at Johnny, but said nothing.

"I mean, come on, Isaac. It was time for somebody to
bring that psycho down. The rest of us didn't want to mess

with Mickey." Johnny shook his head in amazement. "I should have known that it would take the great Isaac Walker to come back here and take Mickey down."

*Lord, give me the words. I don't know how to break this down to him.*

"So what are you planning to do now? You gon' take over the turf Mickey left?"

"Yeah," Isaac told him with a smile. "I plan to take over your territory also, but not the way you think."

Johnny jumped off the car.

"Sit back down," Isaac commanded him.

Johnny obliged, but he scooted farther away from Isaac.

"Look, I'm not out here to kill you and sell your drugs." As he said the words, Isaac could hear the Lord once again telling him, ***I am stronger than your strongman.*** "I want to take over this area by introducing you to a better way."

Johnny stretched out his arms and embraced the ghetto. "This is the only way I know. What else you think I'm gon' do?"

"Have you ever wondered what it would be like to live in peace? To walk in your home and lie in your bed without worrying about some guy killing you while you sleep?"

"Isaac, you know better than I do, that's just a part of the game. You want to hustle, prepare to die young. I'm just trying to live it up before my time comes."

"How long have you known me, Johnny?"

"About ten, fifteen years."

"I've always been straight up with you, haven't I?"

Johnny shrugged. "Yeah. We all know. You real—what you see is what you get with you."

"Then can I tell you a little bit of the truth I know?"

Johnny nodded.

Isaac told Johnny that all hustlers go to hell. And that

many of the guys they ran the streets with are down there
right now, wishing, hoping and screaming to get out. But
there was no out once in. No amount of apologies for not
knowing the truth will save a hustler from his final fate.
Then Isaac told him about God's love and how he could
avoid eternity in hell.

"Man, if this God of yours loves us so much, why is all this
stuff always happening? I mean, you can turn on the news
any given day and babies are dying, homies getting murdered and jacked for everything they got."

"This is a dangerous world we live in, but God did not
make it like this. God gave man the ability to choose. Unfor-
tunately, we choose to pick up a gun faster than we pick up
a Bible." Isaac shrugged. "You can't blame God for that."

"To tell you the truth, when Mickey's rampage started, I
went to The Rock one Sunday."

Isaac smiled heavenward. *God, you have given him to
me, haven't you? Just when I think I'm doing something,
you set me up from the beginning.* "I know the church well.
My son goes there." He didn't mention Nina to Johnny. Their
thing was too new; he was still trying to let it settle.

"The preacher at The Rock sounds just like you. All hell
and brimstones—I had to leave. It messed me up."

"It's true, Johnny. You either serve God while you're living
on earth, or die and live in hell's everlasting torment."

Johnny got off the car. "Man, I don't believe in all that
stuff. But, I'll think about what you said." They clasped
hands again. "I gotta go handle my business."

"All right, man. I'll catch up with you later," Isaac told him
as he watched him walk away. Isaac got back in his car and
then lowered his head and prayed for Johnny. He desperately hoped that he hadn't been too forceful with him; hadn't
run him off before he could really minister to him.

After Johnny was seated in his SUV for a moment, he
rolled down the passenger side window.

Isaac looked up, wondering if he was about to get a bullet for his efforts.

"How 'bout I meet you over at The Rock this Sunday?"

Isaac's phone rang. "I'll see you Sunday. I hear there's going to be a revival over at the new center on James H. McGee."

As Johnny backed out of the parking lot, Isaac answered his cell. It was Bishop Sumler.

"Hey, Isaac, my boy. Have you had time to think about our discussion?" Bishop asked with a hint of optimism in his voice.

Isaac waved at Johnny and mouthed, "I'll see you Sunday," then turned his attention back to his call. "I prayed about it."

"I'm glad to hear it. When will you be back home?"

Isaac hesitated. "I'm not coming back, Bishop. God has sent me in a different direction."

Sumler stuttered. "W-what k-kind of different direction?"

"I'm not totally sure of God's plan for my life right now, but I do know it involves ministering to people like me."

"Well, that's what I've offered you, Isaac. You'll be ministering to thousands."

"I'm talking about street people, Bishop."

He heard the gasp through the phone line. "Why on earth would you want to waste your time with people like that?"

"Because I'm just like them, or at least, I was. They need to see me, so they can believe that God can change their lives too."

"I don't think it's a good idea. There's no one to protect you down there, son. You get yourself into some mess and everyone will know about it."

"That's just it, Bishop. I don't want my sins covered. I want to remember the wrong I've done. I want to have my sins stretched out before God—after all, He is the forgiver of my sins."

"The people won't receive from a pastor who is so openly transparent about his own faults."

"That's the people's problem. I've decided to live this thing for God." Isaac hung up as fat drops of rain began to fall. Wiping a few drops from his face, he jumped in the car. Before taking off, he sat motionless, watching the rain descend. He had learned to hate the rain. It had brought him nothing but sorrow. But that was the former rain that fell into his life. Maybe this rain would bring about a new thing. He rolled down his window as he said aloud, "The rain comes whether we want it or not." Might as well embrace it, he thought while sticking his hand out of the window and letting the drops fall in his palm. Kind of like God holding His people in the palm of His hand. No harm could come when God had His children's backs. This rain would not harm him. Not ever again.

Joy invaded Isaac's space as he drove down the street. He was going home to be with his family. They would have dinner, talk about this new assignment and then pray for direction. Life was simple when in the midst of God's will. Simple, but sweet.

# Epilogue

*Here we go again*, Nina thought as the double doors were opened and the congregation came into view. Her man was standing next to Pastor McKlinley. Keith stood with him also. They were smiling, beckoning her to come forward. Donavan's face was aglow with pride and joy as he held the ring that would soon belong to Nina.

"You ready?"

Nina looked at the flowers in her hand, then at Marvin, as he put his hand around her arm. She turned and looked at Isaac again. He had gone and done it. She couldn't explain it, but the man had dazzled her all over again. "More than you'll ever know," she replied to Marvin's inquiry as they began their jaunt down the aisle. Isaac hadn't forgiven his father yet, but he had managed to have a few civil conversations with him. Isaac hadn't even given Nina a hard time when she told him she wanted Marvin to walk her down the aisle.

Elizabeth softly sang, "You Are the One" by Tonya Baker. Oooos and aaahhhs spread throughout the sanctuary as the guests viewed Nina's ivory, pearl embellished wedding gown.

Lipstick smudged her veil as she told Marvin, "It feels like my legs are about to give out on me."

He smiled at her. "I'll carry you the rest of the way if I have to."

"Thanks, Daddy." The word she'd longed to say. She had been denied that privilege until now. Marrying Isaac would gain her a father-in-law. She remembered how Isaac cringed when she told him that. Oh, well, she thought. Forgiveness was a process. It had taken her years to forgive herself, and already she could tell that Isaac was coming around. Marvin had been walking her down the aisle for a full minute and Isaac hadn't threatened to kill him, not even once. She chuckled inwardly at her own humor, then smiled as she stood next to her future husband.

She wiped his face. *No need for tears, baby. This is all we've ever wanted.*

"I love you," he told her as he lifted the veil. "Always have. Don't plan to stop no time soon."

Now she needed some tissue. Knew she should have taken the wedding photos before she marched down the aisle.

When they were pronounced man and wife, Isaac needed no further instructions. He pulled Nina close and devoured her warm and inviting mouth before God and the entire church. Reluctantly pulling away, he kissed the hand that held his ring. "Thank you, Mrs. Walker."

"What are you thanking me for?" She brushed away a lone tear as it traveled down her husband's handsome face.

"For forgiving me."

He was hers and she was his. Isaac stepped back and breathed a sigh of relief as he watched Nina pose for the photographer. Keith walked over to him with a Louis Vutton briefcase. "Mickey's mom just dropped this off for you."

"What is it?"

Keith smiled. "Open it, man. You're not going to believe this."

Isaac opened the briefcase and ogled at the dollars stacked high inside. A piece of paper on top of the money read, "Congrats on your wedding, Dawg. Hopefully, this money can help you save a few souls—I sure can't use it where I'm going."

Isaac laughed. "That boy is a nut. It's about two hundred and fifty grand in here." He turned back to Keith. "His mom gave her life to the Lord at JC's funeral. I guess she was serious."

Slapping his friend on the back, Keith said, "If she wasn't, you wouldn't have gotten this money. Crack heads don't give money away."

"You know that's right." They high-fived. "I've got plans for this community," he told Keith. "This will sure help get them started." Isaac had no problem using Mickey's money. It might have started out dirty, but Isaac knew first hand that in God's hands, dirty money could be cleansed and used for the kingdom.

Keith's smile was bright as he asked his friend, "So how does it feel to get the woman of your dreams and a quarter of a million all in one day?"

Isaac hunched his shoulders. "Feels kinda weird, like this can't be real. I'm still waiting on the other shoe to drop."

Keith stopped smiling. "Don't look now, but I think the other shoe just dropped."

Isaac closed the briefcase, then turned. Cynda was strutting toward him in those same three-inch heels he'd always hated. She was just as beautiful as always. Those skintight red leather pants weren't called for. But Isaac knew what Cynda's line of work was—he understood the attire.

"Hey, baby," she said as she rubbed Isaac's back, then tried to sneak in a kiss.

Isaac stepped back and looked over to where Nina was standing. She was happily in conversation with Elizabeth.

"What?" Cynda asked sarcastically. "I can't kiss the groom?"

Cynda was a part of his past. A past that he had tried to bury, but now realized he couldn't. He wanted to help her get out of the mess she had fallen into, but there was no way he was going to do that on his wedding day.

"Cynda, you need to leave," Isaac told her.

"Oh, it's like that." Cynda's voice escalated, causing the few people who were left in the sanctuary to turn and stare. "You got who you want, so you don't need Cynda no more. Just throw me out with the trash like you always did."

"I'm not trying to have a confrontation with you today." The last time he'd seen her, she'd spit in his face. He wasn't about to go through another episode like that. He turned to Keith. "Help me out, man. Get her out of here."

Nina came and stood next to Isaac. Cynda turned her venom away from the groom and onto the bride. "You're not perfect. You've done wrong."

"You're right, Cynda. I've done plenty of things wrong in my life. But God has forgiven me. He will forgive you too, if you let Him," Nina said with eyes that implored Cynda to choose the Lord.

Cynda lunged at Nina. Isaac wasn't having that. He grabbed her and shoved her into Keith's arms.

"Forget you and your God, Nina. You ain't nothing special," Cynda screamed at Nina as Keith held her back.

"Get her out of here," Isaac yelled at Keith.

"I hate you, Isaac," Cynda said as Keith pulled her out. "I'm the reason you spent those years in prison. That's right. I turned you in."

Her laughter was a loud and evil echo as Keith carried her out the back door.

"Did she say she was the one who turned me in?" Isaac's fist balled.

Nina put her hand on her husband's shoulder. "Let it go, baby."

Slowly the rage that attempted to run through him subsided. He looked to his new wife. "I need to forgive her, don't I?"

Nina smiled. "Yes, Isaac. Forgive her, and let it go."

With a wicked grin he told her, "I'll think about it."

Davison stood in the outer court of heaven with a host of angels looking down on Isaac and his good thang. Arnoth stepped forward with a heavy heart as he watched Cynda being dragged out of the church.

Captain Aaron put his hand an Arnoth's shoulder. "Don't worry, my friend. She will come around."

"But when, Captain?" Shaking his head, Arnoth said, "I still remember that beautiful little girl I protected. She was so scared when she couldn't find her granny. I sat next to her and told her the story about the lost sheep." He looked at Aaron. "You know, the one that Jesus told while He was on earth. I told her not to worry about being lost because the good Shepherd would leave all ninety nine of His sheep to go out and find the one that was lost."

"Cynda hasn't forgotten what you told her, Arnoth. Go, help her to believe it."

## THE END

# A Note to Readers

Latter Rain is about forgiveness. So, during the course of writing and re-writing this book I encountered situations where I felt unjustly treated, and flat out wronged. I wanted to hold onto feelings of strong dislike and resentment, but God would not allow that. Like the mighty force He is, He not only taught me to love my family, friends and enemies, but to forgive them. Thank you, Lord.

As you read this book, do yourself a favor; let the Lord teach you how to forgive, let go and to not even sweat the BIG stuff. My prayer is that you will put all your problems in God's capable hands and let him fight your battles.

Happy Reading,

Vanessa

*Please turn this page for a bonus excerpt from*

# RAIN STORM

the fourth book in the

# RAIN SERIES

by Vanessa Miller

# Prologue

*And the Lord said to Hosea, Go take unto thee a wife of whoredoms and children of whoredoms: for the land hath committed great whoredom, departing from the Lord.*

Hosea 1:2

Cynda was nine when she decided to hate her mother. Standing above her coffin, watching her grandmother sob and fall apart, she whispered, "I hate you for leaving—for loving that man more than me."

"Hush, child. It's not right to speak so of the dead."

"It's true, Grammy. She was a whore. The kids at school said so. Her pimp killed her because she gave it to somebody for free."

The smack brought tears to her eyes and sent her scampering to sit down and stay in a child's place as Grammy instructed. Sitting in the back of the funeral home, Cynda listened as men and women openly discussed her mother.

"That Flora was some woman."

"Prettiest thing this side of Georgia," a man with teeth so big he looked like he should be chomping down on a carrot said.

"That was before Romie turned her out," a portly woman dressed in a long black dress added.

"I don't care what Romie did to her. I still wanted to be

with that beautiful woman. Something special about Flora—that's for sure."

"Well, all the special done been beat out of her now."

He shook his baldhead. "I hope they give that good-for-nothing the chair."

A mean-spirited laugh escaped the portly woman's mouth. "For killing a whore? Get real."

As Cynda got up, she wished that her grandmother could hear all her mother's so-called friends; maybe she'd back hand each one them too.

"Hey." The portly woman nudged the carrot chomper. "That's her kid."

"Look at the flawless amber skin tone and that long flowing hair. She's going to be more beautiful than Flora ever would have been."

"I hope she likes older men."

The group laughed as though they were at a comedy club. Cynda ran out of the funeral home. Ran down the street, around the corner, and kept on running until she couldn't remember where that awful place had been.

She smiled, until common sense halted her glee and caused her heart to pound. If she couldn't remember where the funeral home was, then she wouldn't be able to get back to her grandmother.

She sat down on the stoop of an abandoned house and began to cry. With tears cascading down her face, Cynda admitted the one thing she had refused to accept since they told her that her mother was dead. She was afraid. Afraid to grow up without her mommy. Afraid to be lost.

A chill went through her when a shadow appeared in front of her. She tried to stop the tears. It wouldn't do to look like a big scared kid in front of a stranger. So she tried to wipe her eyes and look grown up.

But the tears wouldn't stop rolling down her face, so without looking up she asked, "Why are you bothering me? What do you want?"

"I came for you."

Cynda looked up. At first all she saw was a glow—no, more like a big burst of light. She blinked and as the light dimmed, this huge man stood before her. Cynda liked the blinding light better. She blinked again. This man was too big, too scary. As she scooted back a little on the stoop, all she could say was, "Huh?"

"You are lost. Are you not, little one?"

"Why do you want to know? Why are you bothering me?"

"The Good Shepherd sent me."

Scrunching her nose, Cynda asked, "The Good who?"

The strange man sat down next to her. "The Good Shepherd. He sent me here to bring you safely home. You are lost, right?"

Cynda nodded. She saw no harm in admitted what a blind man could see. After all, she had been sitting on this stoop crying like she'd just gotten beaten with three of Grammy's thickest switches.

He reached out his hand to her. "Well, come on, Cynda, your grandmother is frantic with worry."

For some reason Cynda didn't fear this man as she did those bad men who leered at her during the funeral. "How do you know my name?" she asked while putting her small hand in his humongous one.

"The Good Shepherd knows all."

They walked around the corner and up a few blocks. Around another corner and then the strange man lifted his long arm and pointed. Cynda looked down the road and saw her grandmother. She was pacing, looking more mad than worried. Cynda asked, "Why'd this Good Shepherd guy care so much about me?"

"The Good Shepherd loves all that belong to Him. And if

one should get lost, He would leave all the others to go find that one, and restore her to her rightful place."

Okay, she didn't understand all that but, whatever. This nice man had brought her back to her grandmother, and she was no longer lost. She opened her mouth to ask his name, but before she could get the words out, her grandmother screamed for her.

Flailing her arms in the air, Cynda yelled, "I'm right here, Grammy."

Grammy ran toward her. "Oh, thank you, Lord. Thank you." She picked Cynda off the ground and swung her around. "I was so worried about you, chile. Are you all right? How did you find your way back?"

"I'm okay, Grammy. This nice man helped me."

Her grandmother put her down and looked around. "What man, baby?"

Cynda looked around also. "I don't know, Grammy. He was right here. I promise."

She rubbed her granddaughter's shoulder. "That's okay, baby. Let's go home."

# 1

Cynda sat on the edge of the bed, swinging her leg, impatiently waiting for her last customer to get his pants on and leave her alone.

"Woohoo, I tell you what, girl, the half has not been told, about the wonders of your pot of gold."

Great, a poet. Half smiling, Cynda threw his pants at him and glanced at her watch.

"Oh, no you don't. I paid for an hour and I'm getting my whole hour this time. I want to talk."

Rolling her eyes and rubbing her temple usually helped her customers understand that they had over stayed her endurance. But not The Poet. This knucklehead thought his words could sway her, make her change her ways.

The Poet walked around the bed, got on his knees in front of Cynda, and put his hand on her leg. "I want us to be together, baby." Happy fingers traveled up her leg. "You don't have to be out on these streets. Why don't you let me get you a place?"

"So you want your own personal whore, is that it?"

His hand stopped. He stood and turned his back on her. "It wouldn't be like that, Cynda. I want to take care of you."

She got off the king-size bed, squeezed into her red-leather skirt, and bent down to put on her stilettos. "What would your wife say about you taking care of me?"

"I done told you about bringing my wife into this."

Cynda stood and straightened her mini. "Look man, I've got to go. Why don't you go home and spend some of this quality time with your family?"

"Why you always gotta talk trash?"

"Why you always gotta act like a fool?" Throwing on her tank top she grabbed her purse. "Let me ask you this, how much money have you put aside for your son's college expenses while you're making plans to put me up?"

The Poet grabbed his things, then opened the motel door and turned back to face Cynda. "You know something, beautiful outside and ugly inside is a horrible combination."

"Whatever, man. Don't overstay your welcome and you won't see the ugly side of me."

He slammed the door and she sat back on the bed and took the money out of her purse. Between her three customers she'd earned a hundred and fifty dollars. Three years ago, a trick wouldn't have been able to look her way with fifty bucks. Back then, she was racking in three to five hundred per trick. Back then, she did her tricking at four- and five-star hotels. Today, she received her callers at the Motel 6.

Someone knocked on her door. She put her money back in her hand bag and prayed that she wasn't about to get robbed. Not today. She had something important to do with that money. Something real important.

"Who is it?"

"Girl, it's me, Jasmine. Open up this door."

Cynda smiled. Her girl Jasmine was cool people. They'd gotten into some deep stuff that made them call on the name of Jesus. Well, Jasmine called on Jesus, Cynda would rather ask for Satan's help.

The girl was just kicks. Big fun, all the time. Cynda opened the door and Jasmine floated in with Cooper straggling behind.

The two couldn't be a more awkward pair. Where Cooper was tall and lanky, Jasmine was short and well fed. Cooper's cheeks were sunken in, and his face always bore a frown. But Jasmine, that girl put life into the dullest party.

"Girl, I thought your last customer would never leave." Jasmine pulled a bag of weed out of one pocket and some rocks out of the other. "Let's get this party started."

Cynda held up her hand. "I've got to go, Jasmine. I can't get into this right now."

"What you talking 'bout? Girls like us are always ready to party."

"I've gotta get to Spoony's. Today is Iona's birthday."

Jasmine looked at the watch on her swollen wrist. "That girl don't get out of school until three pm. You've got at least an hour before you need to be over there." She put the bags of temptation against Cynda's nostrils and shook them. "What you gon' do?"

Cynda hesitated. But with the bag still under her nose she couldn't concentrate on what she had set her mind to accomplish today. She inhaled and gave in to her desires. "Spread the stuff on the table. I don't have all day; I've got to get going."

Cynda walked out of Motel 6 at five o'clock with ten dollars to her name. The money she made today was supposed to go to Iona. Or better yet, a hundred would go to Spoony for benevolently housing her child, and charging her a thousand dollars a week to do it. She was going to spend the other fifty taking Iona out to eat and picking up a doll for her. But the money went up in smoke from her crack pipe.

Now she stood at Spoony's door shaking like a man headed to the electric chair. Spoony would kill her for blowing that money. Spoony wasn't just her babysitter. Actually he didn't baby sit at all, his loser of a wife Linda did that. Spoony was Cynda's pimp. He'd thrown her out a year ago, but refused to let her daughter go with her. That way, even though he'd stopped housing and clothing her, he was still able to pimp her, because she had to bring him her money in order to see her child. She reminded herself for the thousandth time how bad it was to make deals with the devil.

Cynda rang the door bell and waited. The devil's big, angry feet stomped toward the door and swung it open. "About time you got yourself here. This girl has been waiting on you since she got out of school."

Cynda stepped past the crusty black/blue man who haunted the doorway and smiled at Iona. She was standing in the middle of the living room with one of them frilly white dresses that went out in the 80s. Linda tried her best, but the woman needed to get out more. "Happy birthday, baby." Cynda bent down in front of her daughter and hugged her. She hugged her real tight.

"What did you bring me, Mommy?"

Closing her eyes, Cynda wished for leeches to suck out her blood, while a lion clawed her heart out. Horrible mothers deserved deaths like that, didn't they? She opened her eyes and forced herself to look into her daughter's innocent face. Iona's excited eyes always reminded her of someone else. Someone who didn't want anything to do with her. Someone she'd rather forget. But her daughter looked more like him with every passing day. That smooth chocolate skin and those deep dimples were a signature from the man Cynda refused to think about.

"That's what Mama needs to talk to you about." She nervously rubbed Iona's arms. "See, Mama doesn't have any money right now. I was hoping we could celebrate your birthday this weekend. I'll be able to take you someplace real nice then. Okay?"

"You don't have a present for me, Mama?"

Cynda's heart ached as the excitement seeped out of her daughter's eyes. Where were those leeches? Why didn't her heart explode after she put her daughter's birthday money in a crack pipe? A tear trickled down Cynda's lovely face.

"Don't cry, Mommy." Iona wiped the tear from her mother's face. "Auntie Linda gave me lots of presents. Do you want to see them?"

Auntie Linda was always showing her up. "Not right now, baby. Why don't you get your coat and let Mommy take you to get a slice of pizza."

Spoony grabbed Cynda by the back of her shirt and pulled her up to face him. Snot drizzled from the hairs in his big black nose as he snarled at her. "Where's my money."

Cynda turned to Iona. "Baby, go in the other room with Auntie Linda."

Iona didn't move.

"Where's my money," Spoony asked with his fist looming down on her. "I'm not going to ask you again, Cynda."

"I didn't make any money today." She braced herself for the blow she knew would knock her across the room.

The first lick caused blood to trickle from her lip, and knocked her against black cocktail table. "Iona get out of here!" she screamed before Spoony took a handful of her hair, twisted it around his hand then yanked it as he punched her in the eye.

Iona ran out of the room, whimpering for her aunt.

"You think I can't tell that you smoked up my money?" He threw her on the ground and kicked her with the pointy part of his boot. "It's in your eyes, liar. They're glassy."

Cynda grabbed her rib and forced herself not to cry. "I just want to take my daughter out for a slice of pizza, Spoony. Why do you have to do this on her birthday?"

"She's not going nowhere with you."

"Let me have my kid, Spoony; please. That's all I want from you."

He opened the front door and dragged Cynda toward it, kicking her in the ribs as he threw her out.

Just before slamming the door he told her, "Maybe I should call her daddy and get all that back child support he owes me."

Cynda wanted to spit on him. He always threw that up in her face, reminding her of the secret they shared. The reason she allowed herself to be pimped by this animal. He slammed the door and she was tempted to just leave, never look back. Just forget that Spoony, the devil, existed. But her daughter was still in there. And it was her birthday. Cynda pounded on the door and pleaded with Spoony to let Iona come with her. But her attempts fell on deaf ears. With tears streaming down her face she stood and straightened her clothes. As she walked down the steps, a searing pain shot through her. She sat down and lifted her shirt. Her chest was black and blue. Spoony messed up everything. Didn't he know that birthday's were important to little girls? She still remembered her last birthday spent with her mother. She'd been left outside knocking then too.

"Mama, please let me in." Knocking harder on the door, Cynda said, "Come on, you know it's my birthday."

Footsteps thudded toward the door.

"Do you hear me, Mama? I want to open my presents now."

Flora wiped the sleep from her light brown eyes as she inched the door open. "Hey, baby. You know I've got company right now."

"Are we going to have a party today?"

Flora touched her daughter's smooth young face. "No, baby. Mama, has to work today."

"But we always have a party on my birthday. You always get me lots of presents."

Flora's head bowed low as Romie walked into the hallway. His big Jackson Five afro swayed this way and that as he stalked toward them.

He asked Cynda, "Are you bothering your mother? She's busy."

She backed away from him. His beady black eyes terrified her. "But it's my birthday," Cynda whined.

Romie grabbed her arm. "Come with me, baby girl. I've got a present for you."

"No! No!" Cynda pulled away from him and barreled into her mother, pushing Flora backward into the bedroom. The smell of must wafted in the air. "Don't let him take me, Mama, please."

Flora's eyes widened as she looked from her daughter to Romie. There was a man in Flora's bed. He sat up, pulled the cover over his naked body. "What's going on, Flora?"

"Nothing Ralph, just go back to sleep."

Romie barked, "You don't have time to be fooling around with this child. You need to be making some money."

Flora reached into the pocket of her rob and pulled out several bills. She threw them in Romie's high-yellow face. "Here, is that enough money. Now, can I please spend a few minutes with my daughter on her birthday?"

Fire flashed in Romie's eyes as he smacked Flora. He then grabbed a handful of her long black hair and pulled her close to him. "Don't make me beat you this morning."

Flora put her hands up. "Okay, b-baby, calm down."

He grabbed Cynda's hand. "I am calm. You get back over there and handle Ralph. I'll take Cynda with me."

Birthday's stopped being special for Cynda when her mother stopped standing up for her. Today, she had done the same to her daughter.

# About the Author

Vanessa Miller of Dayton, Ohio is an *Essence* magazine best-selling author. She is also a playwright and motivational speaker. Her stage productions include: **Get You Some Business, Don't Turn Your Back on God, Can't You Hear Them Crying** and **Abundant Rain.** Vanessa is currently in the process of turning all the novels in the Rain Series into stage productions.

Vanessa has been writing since she was a young child. When she wasn't reading, writing poetry, short stories, stage plays and novels consumed her free time. However, it wasn't until she committed her life to the Lord in 1994 that she realized all gifts and anointing come from God. She then set out to write redemption stories that glorified God.

To date, Vanessa has written the Rain Series and the Storm Series. The books in the Rain Series are: **Former Rain**, **Abundant Rain,** and **Latter Rain**. The books in the Storm Series are: Rain Storm and Through the Storm. These books have received rave reviews, winning Best Christian Fiction Awards and topping numerous bestseller's lists. Vanessa believes that each book in The Rain and Storm Series will touch readers in a special way. It is, after all, her God-given destiny to write and produce plays and novels that bring deliverance to God's people.

Vanessa self-published her first three books, then in 2006 she signed a five-book deal with Urban Christian/Kensington. Her books can now be found in Wal-Mart, mostl major bookstores, including African-American bookstores, and online bookstores such as Amazon.com.

Vanessa is a dedicated Christian and devoted mother. She graduated from Capital University with a degree in Organizational Communication. In 2007 Vanessa was ordained by her church as an exhorter, which of course, Vanessa believes was the right position for her because God has called her to exhort readers and to help them rediscover their place with the Lord.

A perfect day for Vanessa is one that affords her the time to curl up with a good book. She is currently working on a new novel outside of the Rain and Storm series. She is also preparing the stage production for the **Former Rain** novel. Go to: *www.vanessamiller.com* for more info on Vanessa and her books.

# Latter Rain

*Vanessa Miller*

## Reading Group Guide

## Isaac

1. Although Isaac's intentions were pure, he failed to balance the needs of his son with his ministry. As a result, Donavan went astray. What does the Word tell us about raising our children?

Proverbs 22:6, 15          Ephesians 6:1-4
Proverbs 29:15             Colossians 3:21
Malachi 4:5-6              I Timothy 5:8
I Timothy 3:5

_____

_____

_____

_____

2. Isaac repented of his sins and sought God for forgiveness. When we surrender to the Lord, what can we expect in return?

II Chronicles 7:14         Luke 7:41-50
Psalm 86:5                 Acts 3:19
Psalm 103:3, 12            Colossians 1:12-14
Isaiah 43:25
Isaiah 44:22
Jeremiah 31:34

_____

_____

_____

_____

3. Since God is just, He granted Isaac forgiveness of all his past sins. Yet Isaac struggled with forgiving others. What does the New Testament teach about forgiveness?

| | |
|---|---|
| Matthew 6:14-15 | Luke 12:48 |
| Matthew 18:21-22 | Luke 17:3-4 |
| Mark 11:25-26 | Ephesians 4:31-32 |
| Luke 6:37 | Colossians 3:10-14 |

_____

_____

_____

_____

_____

4. Isaac chose to serve God rather than money, when he rejected Bishop Sumler's lucrative offer. Like Jesus, he chose to minister in the streets rather than a lavish sanctuary. How does the Word support his decision?

| | |
|---|---|
| Isaiah 61:1-2 | Luke 11:37-44 |
| Matthew 6:33-34 | Luke 14:16-24 |
| Matthew 9:9-13 | Acts 3:62 |
| Mark 2:13-17 | I Thessalonians 5:14-24 |

_____

_____

_____

_____

_____

## Nina Lewis

1.      The Bible tells us that once we seek the Lord for forgiveness, He no longer remembers our sin. Oftentimes, we hold ourselves captive by not releasing the very thing we sought the Lord to forgive. How can we forgive ourselves?

Psalm 51                    Romans 3:10, 23
Psalm 103                   Romans 5:1-5
Proverbs 24:16

_____

_____

_____

_____

_____

2.  In an effort to provide Donavan with a stable home, Nina was willing to marry a man that she did not truly love. What does the Word say about trusting God?

II Samuel 22:1-7            Psalm 91
Job 13:15                  Proverbs 3:4-5
Psalm 5:11-12              Isaiah 40:31
Psalm 71                   Hebrews 11:1

_____

_____

_____

_____

_____

## Bishop Sumler

1. Instead of being a man of the cloth, Bishop Sumler was a man hiding behind the cloth. He willfully manipulated others for financial gain. What does the Bible say about manipulation and greed?

   Psalm 52:1-5                    Matthew 6:19-21
   Jeremiah 23:25-27               Matthew 12:35
                                   Mark 12:38-40
                                   Colossians 3:1-3
                                   James 1:22-27

   _____
   _____
   _____
   _____

2. Bishop Sumler created his own code of conduct to have the appearance of holiness. His self-righteousness can be compared to that of the scribes and Pharisees. What do the scriptures teach us about having the form of godliness?

   Proverbs 23:7                   Matthew 15:8
   Proverbs 30:12-13               Matthew 16:1-12
   Isaiah 29:13                    Matthew 23
   Isaiah 64:4                     Mark 7:1-13
                                   Luke 20:45-47
                                   II Timothy 3:1-6

   _____
   _____
   _____
   _____

3. As a prodigy of Bishop Sumler, Pastor Ron Marks took
   on his character. Instead of humility, he was full of pride.
   How does God feel about pride?

   Psalm 10:4-18              Proverbs 8:13
   Psalm 73:6-9               Proverbs 16:18
   Psalm 131:1-3              Daniel 4:37
   Proverbs 6:16-19           I Timothy 3:1-7
                              I John 2:15-17

   _____

   _____

   _____

   _____

   _____


4. What expectations has God established for church lead-
   ers?

   Ephesians 5:27             Titus 1:5-16
                              Titus 2:1-8

   _____

   _____

   _____

   _____

   _____

## **General**

1.  God desires that we walk in His perfect, not permissive, will. What is God's will for our lives?

    Psalm 37:23                    I Thessalonians 5:18
    Psalm 119:133                  I Peter 3:17-18
    Isaiah 64:8                    I Peter 5:1-14
    John 4:31-34
    John 7:16-18
    I Thessalonians 4:3-7

    _____
    _____
    _____
    _____
    _____

2.  God wants us to worship Him from our heart, so He gave us a will. How do we as believers line up with His plan?

    Genesis 12:1-3                 Mark 14:36
    Deuteronomy 28:1-14            John 5:30
    Joshua 1:8                     Romans 8:6-13
    Isaiah 55:6-13                 Colossians 3:5-9
    Jeremiah 1:4-10

    _____
    _____
    _____
    _____
    _____

# Urban Christian His Glory Book Club!

Established January 2007, *UC His Glory Book Club* is another way by which to introduce to the literary world, Urban Book's much-anticipated new imprint, **Urban Christian** and its authors. We are an online book club supporting Urban Christian authors by purchasing, reading and providing written reviews of the authors' books that are read. *UC His Glory* welcomes both men and women of the literary world who have a passion for reading Christian based fiction.

*UC His Glory* is the brainchild of Joylynn Jossel, Author and Executive Editor of Urban Christian and Kendra Norman-Bellamy, Author and Copy Editor for Urban Christian. The book club will provide support, positive feedback, encouragement and a forum whereby members can openly discuss and review the literary works of Urban Christian authors. In the future, we anticipate broadening our spectrum of services to include: online author chats, author spotlights, interviews with your favorite Urban Christian author(s), special online groups for *UC Book Club* members, ability to post reviews on the website and amazon.com, membership ID cards, *UC His Glory* Yahoo Group and much more.

Even though there will be no membership fees attached to becoming a member of *UC His Glory Book Club,* we do expect our members to be active, committed and to follow the guidelines of the Book Club.

*UC His Glory* **members pledge to:**
- Follow the guidelines of *UC His Glory Book Club.*
- Provide input, opinions, and reviews that build up, rather than tear down.

- Commit to purchasing, reading and discussing featured book(s) of the month.
- Agree not to miss more than three consecutive online monthly meetings.
- Respect the Christian beliefs of *UC His Glory Book Club*.
- Believe that Jesus is the Christ, Son of the Living God

We look forward to the online fellowship.

**Many Blessings to You!**

**Shelia E Lipsey**
**President**
**UC His Glory Book Club**

**\*\*Visit the official Urban Christian Book Club website at <u>www.uchisglorybookclub.net</u>**